Something to Hide

Books by Nicholas Monsarrat

NICHOLAS

*

SOMETHING
TO HIDE

MONSARRAT

A William Sloane Associates Book
Published by
William Morrow & Company, Inc.
New York   1966

Something to Hide

*

1

Carter saw the girl from a long way away, as one always could on a clear evening, with the sun behind one's head slanting down the highway. Even at a distance, she was a forlorn figure, picking her way painfully along the grass edge, turning her head briefly as the car ahead of his whipped past, then turning back again to plod onwards; and as his own car drew near, he saw that she was indeed forlorn.

She was limping; her shabby coat flapped around her bare legs like a flag of surrender; her long yellow hair hung limply across her shoulders. Just before he passed her, she turned again, and signaled hopelessly, and he had a glimpse of a pale, pasty face, and a mouth open, saying something, calling out something. A hitchhiker, a girl down on her luck. . . . He thought, as he usually did: Why should I stop? and then, for no reason at all save pity, he changed his mind.

Against his better judgment (since hitchhikers sometimes pulled out guns and turned into bandits, and girls made trouble anyway), he braked, and drew his car onto the gravel, and waited for her to catch him up.

It took a little time, because she walked heavily and awkwardly, and she was obviously bone-weary; his distaste grew as he saw what he had stopped for. She did not look like a bandit, but she did look like a nuisance; a girl running away from home, a girl escaping from a reformatory, a girl no one wanted anymore. . . . He would have started his car again, and left her flat-footed; but by now he felt ashamed to, and in a moment it was too late.

Carter opened the opposite door as she drew level. Close to, she looked like a real loser. The pallid face, framed by the overload of yellow hair, was thin and pinched; her flapping coat was threadbare and stained by the weather, and her sharp-pointed shoes, once white, were cracked and scuffed to a dirty grey.

She had never even been pretty, he decided, with sudden impatience and dislike; now she was a mess, and he was stuck with her, on that silly kind of impulse which made other men give their loose change to street-corner drunks, or rescue stranded cats from trees, or vote for the underdog. . . . But he need not be stuck for long.

He said briefly: "Want a lift?" and she bent and peered at him, not smiling, not changing her expression, and answered "O.K.," and climbed awkwardly into the front seat. She could have said "Thank you," thought Carter, irritated again, as he put the car into low gear and edged over onto the highway. Of all the people he might have stopped for, it was just his luck to pick an ugly girl who didn't say thank you.

The girl sighed heavily as she settled in, and then slumped back and let her head fall to one side, as if she were going to sleep. Wonderful, thought Carter, working through his gears till he was up to traffic speed again; now I'm running the sleeping-car service. . . . More out of annoyance than anything else, he asked, rather loudly:

"Where are you heading for?"

She must have been alert, in spite of her dead-alive air, because she answered straightaway: "Down the road. As far as you're going."

It sounded too vague for comfort, and too binding at the same time. *Whither thou goest, I will go,* he thought, and reacted immediately, defensively.

"I've only got another thirty miles."

"O.K.," she answered indifferently. "Thirty miles is fine."

"The next town is Stampville."

"O.K.," she said again. "Stampville."

"Is that where you want to go?"

"Not that I know of."

He let two faster cars pass him before he asked, still trying for some sort of communication: "Don't you live around here?"

"No."

"Where are you going, then?"

"Down the road. Like I said."

He glanced sideways, and saw that her eyes were now closed, and her hands folded in her lap, in a manner so settled, so resigned, that he grew wary again. At this rate, it wouldn't be long before he was *really* stuck with her. He tried, once more, to sort out the riddle.

"Are you looking for a job? Is that it?"

She opened her eyes, and jerked upwards. "Questions!" she shot back, with sudden, surprising venom. "Every time, questions! All I want from you is a lift. O.K.?"

"All right," he said, and smiled in spite of his annoyance. She really was a dead loss, but he had known this sort of savage mood in himself and could recognize it. "No more questions, then. You've got yourself a lift."

"O.K."

It was grudging, and sulky, but at least it closed off the scene. The girl relaxed again, as if sure that she had made her point, and Carter went back to his driving.

He drove slowly and carefully, as he always did; it was all that his shabby, seven-year-old car was good for. Once or twice he glanced at the girl, and then glanced no more, because there was really nothing to see. She seemed to be asleep, and with sleep the pallid, featureless face had grown younger, shedding some of its sulky toughness, some of its defenses.

Her true age, he decided, was probably not more than sixteen. But she had not become any prettier, for all this softening process; she remained what she had been when he picked her up—a dull girl, an ugly girl, a girl unloved and probably unloving.

He could feel sorry for her, but not too sorry. It did not matter, now, that he had wasted his time and trouble giving her a lift; but he was glad that he would soon be rid of her. It had just been a silly thing to do; one of those silly things that needed to be put right, as soon as the chance came up.

She slept, and he drove, all in silence. Once she stirred, with a sharp movement, and her hands in her lap tightened protectively, in a way which reminded him of something—but the something slipped away before he could identify it.

It took him nearly an hour to get to Stampville, and dusk was falling as he slowed for the outskirts of the town. The change in the engine-note must have woken her, for he presently noticed that she was sitting up, and her eyes were open.

"Stampville," he said, in explanation.

She looked around her, rather warily, taking in the street lamps, the shops closed for the night, the thin traffic of the market town.

"This where you live?"

"No," answered Carter. "I'm about five miles further on. Along by the river."

She nodded, and seemed ready to settle down again. It was not what he had planned, and he said, as firmly as he could:

"I'd better drop you off here. If you want to go on,

you've more chance of picking up a lift somewhere in town."

"Where?" she asked.

"I don't know," he answered shortly. "One of the service stations, maybe."

"Why can't I go on with you?"

"It's only five miles more."

"Five miles is five miles. When you're walking."

"But you might be walking all night."

"I'll find something."

He opened his mouth again, ready with another argument, and then he changed his mind. The more he argued, the more he could become entangled, caught up in her problems. The quickest way was to take her as far as he could, and then cut the thing off, with good reason and no alternative.

He said indifferently: "Have it your own way," and shifted gear for the approaching corner, and drove on out of town again.

Five miles was five miles, as she had said; a weary trudge for walkers, a ten-minute breeze even in a slow car. Presently he was easing down again, preparing to stop; and as he did so the girl made a curious sound, half a groan, half a sob, and turned her face away from him as if she were trying to go into hiding.

"Are you all right?" asked Carter, deliberately unimpressed.

"Sure." But she was shivering, and her voice had tightened, as if it were now an effort to speak. "Sure. I'm O.K."

The car rolled to a halt, beside a line of half-a-dozen rural mailboxes, and a gravel track leading down into trees.

"This is my turnoff," said Carter with finality. He really must close this thing up before it got out of hand. If she was ill, then she was ill, and shouldn't be walking around and hitching lifts. He wasn't a doctor, and he didn't intend to set up in practice, on this or any other night. "I'll say good-bye."

There was a long silence, broken by a big truck thundering past at high speed, rocking his car as the shock wave of its advance hit them. The girl sat where she was, tense, withdrawn, staring straight ahead of her into the dusk, perhaps summoning up the courage to get out and face it. He was not surprised, only annoyed, to hear her say:

"Can't I stay?"

"No," he answered curtly. "That's not possible."

"Why not?"

"The answer is no."

"Just for the night," she said. "I'll sleep outside, in the car, if you like."

"No," he said again. "That wasn't the deal, and

you know it. You wanted a lift, I gave you a lift. This is where it stops."

"I need help," she said suddenly, violently. "You've got to help me."

"I haven't got to do anything."

He reached across, prepared to push open the door, prepared to do anything to be rid of her; and as he did so, her hands lifted and she threw open her loose coat in a curious gesture of revelation—like a salesgirl, like a lecturer demonstrating.

During that split second of warning, he had been expecting many things—a scream, a pantomime of assault, a wild physical appeal, even nakedness—and his frightened mind, running ahead, had been ready to deal with them. But he had never expected what he now saw. Under the flapping disguise of the coat was a cheap, wrap-around skirt and a bulging smock; and under the smock a girl who, clearly, could not carry her child for very much longer.

She watched him as his glance took in the facts—the facts of life. She gave him time to be jolted. Then she said, in a harsh, almost accusing voice:

"I told you. You've got to help me."

*

2

Carter did not really begin to think again, in any co-
herent sense, until he and the girl were inside his
house, and the curtains drawn, and his privacy—
their privacy—secured. Until then, all he had to goad
him was a series of swift, scary snapshots of what
might happen if he did *not* give her shelter. They
had started from the moment she said: "You've got to
help me."

He could push her out of his car, and she would

have her child by the roadside, and it would be dead, and the girl as well, and it would all be charged to him, and the words "BRUTAL ABANDONMENT" would be there for everyone to see, in large black type. . . . He could take her to a hospital, and see her through an area vaguely labeled "ADMITTING," and thus get rid of her—until a large and formidable woman in a white uniform asked him: "Mr. Carter, what is your relationship to the—ah—mother-to-be?"

He could drive her a few miles further on, and there eject her, and be clearly seen in the headlights of another car, arguing loudly, using force. . . . He could deliver her to the nearest police station, and hand her over, and then, just as he was leaving, the sergeant—again a large and formidable character—would say, deliberately: "Just a minute, you! Do you usually pick up sixteen-year-old girls on the road at night?"

He could get rid of her in any other way, and still be involved. He could give her money, and later try to explain why. He could buy her a bus-ticket, and then be identified as the last man to see her alive. He could, out of the goodness of his heart, escort her into the lobby of a hotel, and a week later a police-man would walk right into the town hall where he worked, and say, in front of everyone: "Carter, we know you took her to this hotel. *But why did you leave her there?*"

He could do any of these things, and somehow escape notice, and still be cornered by a blackmailing brother following fast behind.

For all sorts of reasons, he did not want to get involved any deeper than he was already. It was quite enough, it was more than enough. . . . He had a job to keep, a small reputation to preserve, a preference for peace and quiet, a dislike of the police. For all sorts of reasons, it was easier to do as she asked, and take her in. Just for the moment, just till he could sort the thing out.

That was as far as his thoughts had brought him, when they stood and faced each other in the curtained room. He did not even know if he was safe now; though it was dusk, someone might have seen her getting out of the car, going up the pathway to the house. They were always watching his house for girls, ever since his wife went away. Good neighbours, nice people. . . . A man could live alone in a small house on the river bank, with his nearest neighbour a hundred yards away, and still do every damned thing under the limelight.

That was as far as he had thought, except to recall, with sick anxiety, what she had said when they were getting out of the car. He had asked when the baby was due, and she had answered almost jauntily, as if it did not matter one way or the other now that she was sure of shelter for a little longer:

"I guess, any time."

Any time. . . . Watching her as she stood in the middle of the room, her coat off, he could believe it. It was something he knew absolutely nothing about, something he had only encountered in domestic-crisis routines on television, or in newspaper stories about babies being born in cabs ("STORK WINS RACE"); he was lost, and thus entirely vulnerable to the sort of panicky pressure which had made him waver, and then retreat, in the first place.

He had said, then, that she could "come in for a bit"; now she was in, and clearly it was going to be much more difficult to get her out again than it had ever been in the car. Unless he thought of something quickly, she would be staying the night—that much was obvious; and at the moment he could think of nothing except that, for the first time in more than a year, he had a girl in his house, and this time the girl was pregnant and, seemingly, destitute, and he did not even know who she was.

With some idea of regularizing things, of catching up with the normality he felt he must regain, he said:

"I'm Jack Carter."

It sounded slightly ridiculous even as he said it, but, apparently, only to him. The girl, who was looking around the room with quick, calculating glances, answered offhand:

"I'm Jo-Anne Broom."

He hesitated. "Is that Mrs. Broom?"

"Are you kidding?"

The grimace which passed across her face as she answered him was really one of the most unpleasant things he had ever seen. It seemed to express, in a fleeting moment, all the things she was not—not married, not protected, not safe from the world and its cruelties, not part of anything that counted; and, at the same time, it told of other things in her mind which he could only guess at—her rage at the society of squares which had her on the run, the sisterhood of other, prettier girls who somehow managed to make it to the altar, practically as good as new, the boy or man who had done this to her, and then chickened out.

Carter was, indeed, only guessing; he was over forty, and could not know the jargon of revolt; but there had been a look on her face as she asked derisively: "Are you kidding?" which gave him something like a peephole into hell, where the losers sneered upwards at the only thing they had to mock—the pious masks of the winners. . . . He would never reach this ugly, lost girl, and he could be glad of it. But that, once again, did not solve the problem which was his own, here and now. This girl was not quite lost, because he had given her a reprieve. She was under his roof, and likely to stay there until he pushed her out again.

He seemed further than ever away from this as she sat down on the long sofa by the fireplace, and put her feet up, and asked:

"How about you?"

"What do you mean?" he asked.

She gestured around the room. "Are you on your own? Aren't you married?"

"Yes. But my wife's away."

"Oh." Across her face passed another grimace, unpleasant like the last one, corrupt, knowing. "Then it's all right, then."

She was settling in, on her own crude terms— she even *sounded* settled—and he did not like it.

"It's not all right at all," he answered tartly. "I don't have girls staying the night here."

"What's the matter with you?"

He ignored it. "Haven't you got anyone to help you? Any family?"

"I wouldn't be on the road if I did."

"On the road from where?"

"Home."

"Where's home?"

"Why should I tell you?" Suddenly she was glaring at him. "You're not interested. You just want to get rid of me. Like everyone else."

"I don't want to get rid of you," he protested. "Not like that. But this thing doesn't make any sense. You must have *somebody* besides me to help you. What about the—you know, the father?"

She pulled another face, one in which contempt and hatred were evenly mixed. "He's a creep. The creep of creeps."

"But he's responsible."

"Oh sure, he's responsible, all right. About a million miles away, he's responsible. He took off."

"And your family?"

"They don't want to know."

"So you're running away."

"Yes." And as she saw the look on his face: "Where have you been living?" she demanded scornfully. "Lots of girls run away. Lots of girls have to. It isn't the end of the world, for them or anyone else. It's just all there is to do."

"But running, where to?"

"Like I said. Down the road. That's why I flagged you for a lift."

They were not getting anywhere, Carter realized; no solutions were in sight, no answers to problems which, though as old as time itself, were very new, very pressing, when they landed on your own front doorstep. An hour earlier, it seemed, Jo-Anne Broom had been entirely friendless; now she had a friend, a chance-come, unwilling friend, who had somehow been maneuvered into the part, and was stuck with it. It was the very last thing he needed, and that didn't solve any problems either.

Carter looked at the girl. She was lying back on the sofa, her eyes closed; her face was pale, drawn, a mirror of exhaustion and despair. He wanted nothing more to do with her, and yet she was there. Once he had stopped for her, she had climbed right in—into his car, into his house, into his life.

Perhaps he had better deal with one thing at a time.

"When did you eat last?" he asked.

"Yesterday."

"We'd better fix some supper, then."

"You want me to cook it?"

"No."

"Just as well." Her eyes opened, and her mouth curled into a smirk which invited anyone within reach to slap it as hard as he could. "I don't cook."

Carter, making for the kitchen, suppressed a sigh. He was beginning to understand why the father, that creep of creeps, had taken off. This was a young man to be envied, even commended. Responsible or not, he had shown some commonsense. . . . A million miles was not too much to put between oneself and this really horrible girl.

It must have been true that she had not eaten that day; he had never seen a girl so hungry, so ravenous, a girl who fell on her food as if it would be snatched away unless she snatched it for herself. She wolfed everything he set before her, everything on the table—scrambled eggs and bacon, cheese, toast, butter, jam, a hunk of salami sausage, half a jar of pickles; she gulped down three cups of coffee, finished off a carton of milk, dipped slices of bread in a saucer of tomato ketchup and swallowed them with noisy relish. . . . He did not try to keep up with her, nor was it necessary; this was not a social occasion, it was more like famine relief and, as such, outside all the normal rules.

When she had finished stoking up—there was no other phrase to be used—and had made a slap-dash effort at piling the dishes, and none at all at washing them, she settled down on the sofa again, an adopted stray who was quickly carving a permanent niche for herself. But, with hunger stayed, she was more amenable; and when Carter began to question her again, the answers came easily enough. She was not greatly improved, but at least she had shed some of her earlier, total resentment; she was, by a small margin, easier to put up with.

Jo-Anne Broom was seventeen—his first guess had been nearly right. She came from "back there" (she gestured vaguely westwards) but she would not name a town, nor give any other clue. "What's the use?" she asked him, offhand. "There's nothing for me there. I won't be going back."

"Why not?"

"Would you go back? . . . They all know me. And anyway—"

"Anyway what?"

"My folks pushed me out."

"When was that?"

"'Bout three months ago. When—you know."

"When they found out?"

"When *he* found out. My father."

"What does your father do?"

"He's a minister. What else?" Momentarily her lips curled, reflecting the earlier mood of snarling contempt. "Peace on earth. Good will to men. Love one another. But don't get yourself pregnant."

Carter had a curious feeling that she had rehearsed the bitter words, perhaps many times; but he could not pinpoint his suspicion, and he let it go. He had more to find out, before he could sift the truth from the lies.

"What about your mother?"

"She does what she's told." This time the answer was more spiritless, as if here lay a greater disappointment, a more brutal setback. Had this been the real betrayal which had sent a desperate girl off down the road? But Jo-Anne's next words seemed to deny this. "She wouldn't have done different, anyway. It's the way she thinks. It's the way she talks. Go out on dates. Be popular. Get yourself a boy. Promise him anything. *Give him nothing.* . . ." She sighed, theatrically, but she was sighing for something real. "It doesn't work out that way. Boys don't come around for nothing. They come around to collect, and if you say no, you don't win any prizes. You just lose the boy."

"You lost him anyway," said Carter, without too much thought.

"Well, thanks!" she snapped back. "You're a great help."

"I mean," said Carter, "if you're going to lose him anyway, you might as well say no."

"Try saying no when you're out with a football player."

"Is that how it happened?"

"Sort of. You know—we wrestled."

"Was that the first time?"

"Yes. And the last."

"Where was it?"

"In his car. Where else?"

The picture was complete, or nearly so; it was sad, sordid, and (Carter supposed) fairly commonplace. This was what happened to lots of girls, if the newspapers and magazines were to be trusted, and perhaps it happened to ugly girls more often than to pretty girls; since the ugly ones had a harder time latching on to the available men, they had to give more for less. . . . There was only one gap in her story, and he asked her about it now.

"What about the last three months? Since you left home. What's been happening?"

"Nothing much. I just kept moving on."

"But didn't you have any plans?"

"No. What's the use of plans? . . . I had a couple of jobs. Working in motels. But they weren't any good. And pretty soon . . . You just have to keep moving, that's all. Something's bound to happen. Or you meet someone. You know—like you." She looked up at him, critically, boldly, with the first display of personal interest she had shown; and Carter decided there and then that he would rather have her keep to the earlier version. "What do you do, anyway?"

"I work at the town hall. In Stampville."

"Gee—a politician?"

"No. In the valuation department. Properties, assessments, that sort of thing. I was coming back from looking at a farm when I—met you."

"Sure was a stroke of luck for me. . . . Gee!" she said again. "I didn't know you were a big shot like that. But why don't you get yourself a new car? Ride around a little, live it up. You're not too old, you know."

"I don't want a new car."

"If you took those glasses off you'd be just fine. For anyone."

She was smiling now, a thin yet inviting little smile; it made her face, her whole manner, seem utterly corrupt. The approach, which was unmistakable, revolted Carter, and he reacted very quickly. He said: "I'm going to check up outside," and went swiftly out of the room, and out of the house.

There, he did take off his glasses, and drew a deep and grateful breath of the warm night air, and blessed —as he had a thousand times before—the peace of the river at night. The few feet of his front lawn sloped down to the water's edge; in the early moonlight, he could just make out the wooden dock, and the bed of reeds near it; beyond that, the broad river grew grey, and then black, and vanished into the darkness. There were fish still rising, breaking surface with solemn persistence, and a rustle of breeze from the willow tree; all else was silence, and the few lights showing were clean, and friendly, and far away.

He had gone out of the house in anger and disgust, but such a mood could not last; the night was too gentle, the river too beautiful, the small sounds of twilight too reassuring. No girl, however crude, however awful, could spoil this sort of tranquillity. And he could see that, whatever the past, her behaviour *now* was not her fault. She had been on the run for months, with punishment catching up all the time; all she knew of life was the way it had hit her, and the only weapons she had left were her helplessness, and her miserable, marginal appeal to men.

He could be sorry for her. She was near the end of her road; an outcast, a hunted animal carrying the worst burden of all. He could feel pity even as he felt disgust. She was contemptible, and cheap, and coarse; but someone must have wanted her once, if only for five minutes. Let it be his good deed to prolong those five minutes for a few hours more. It would cost him nothing, it could not get him into trouble.

Presently, much more easy in his mind, he went back into the house. She was still sitting where he had left her, on the sofa, relaxed, just as much at home as he.

"Hi!" she said pertly. "I thought you'd taken off."

"I'm going to bed," he told her. "If you want to

stay the night, that's all right with me. But you'll have to get out in the morning."

"O.K.," she said. "Just so as I know."

"There's only one bedroom. You'll have to sleep here. I'll get you a blanket."

"O.K." She was smiling again, though less pleasantly. "I can take a hint."

He might have become angry again, but he let it go. She could not help it, she could not help anything. . . . The price of his compassion was very small, and tomorrow would cancel it out.

*

3

Tomorrow did not cancel anything out. Carter had to leave the house early, as always—his office in the town hall opened at eight, and he was not in any position to be late; and the girl was barely awake by the time he had finished his breakfast. When he came into the living room from the kitchen, she was just beginning to yawn and stretch on the sofa; above the edge of the blanket, her face, swollen and ugly with sleep, peered out at him like a pallid, belated sunrise.

It was a beautiful June morning, but only outside the house. He wanted nothing more than to be rid of her forever.

"Time you got up," he told her curtly.

"O.K., O.K. . . ." Her voice was a sulky mumble. "What's the rush?"

"I have to go to work, and I wasn't aiming to leave you here."

She yawned again, splitting her face into two shapeless halves. It was no improvement. "Think I'll steal something? Is that it?"

"I don't know what you'll do. But you said—we agreed that you were going today."

"I'll go. Just give me time."

"All right." He did not like the idea of leaving her in possession, but there was nothing to be done about it; he could hardly deal with her before he left —pull her off the sofa, put her out of the house and onto the road, all in broad daylight. "When you're ready, just go, that's all. And keep out of sight till you *are* ready. Don't answer the door. Nor the telephone. Just get dressed, and take off."

"What a lot of orders. . . . Can I have a bath?"

"I suppose so."

"Thanks a million."

"Well, God damn it!" he said, irritated, "I did let **you** stay the night."

"Big deal. . . . What d'you want me to do?—kneel down and kiss your hand?"

"Just go, that's all," he repeated.

"I'm on my way."

Of course, she was not on her way—in fact, she had drawn up the blanket again, so that her face was hidden—but he had to leave her, and the situation, where they were. He had no choice, in a corner of the world which kept country hours. Already cars were passing, small boats were moving on the river, and the world was wide awake; he could no longer take a safe hand in her exit. He must trust her to do as she had said, and let her alone to do it.

There was nothing much to steal, anyway.

Carter worked all day, at his dull dusty job in the dull dusty office; the blinds were lowered against the bright sun, putting the whole room into a drab, permanent twilight; when he went out for his lunch, and afterwards sauntered down the main street of Stampville, the people who were carelessly moving in and out of the sunlight—loafers, late-shopping housewives, tourists buying postcards and fishing-tackle, even the policemen watching the parking meters—seemed to him the luckiest people in the world. What it must be like to be really free!—free of daily routine, free of the clock, free of other human beings. . . . But when he examined this thought, this discontent, he knew that it was false.

None of these men and women on the street were really free, any more than he was. Loafers were broke, and therefore worried; housewives had to hurry home to hatch out the baby's formula; tourists had only two more days left of their vacation; policemen were as regimented, as time-pressured, as the meters they were detailed to watch—they were, after all, only an extension of the mechanism. . . . Presently, when the big clock struck the half hour, he went back slowly into his office, reconciled as usual to facing another afternoon among the files and the figures.

Life was dull, but there were always compensations, even in Stampville. At five o'clock, he would be free as anyone he had seen that day; free in his own small house, free to swim in the river, free to fish for his supper, free of that awful girl.

She greeted him as soon as he entered. "Hi!" she said, almost gaily. "The wage earner!" She was lying on the sofa, crudely displayed, alarmingly real. She might never have moved since he left the house, ten hours earlier.

Instantly he was very angry, in one of those spasms of rage which were dangerous, which often got men into trouble. Such a feeling, brutal and overwhelming, had betrayed him before, and he did his best to master it. But his voice was very rough as he said:

"What are you doing here?"

She was eyeing him carefully, gauging his mood. "You asked me in. Remember?"

"Don't fool around!" he snapped. "I told you to get out as soon as you were dressed."

"I couldn't. I felt lousy all morning. I had to lie down."

"You didn't lie down the whole day."

"Nearly. And then someone came to the door."

Carter was quickly alert. "Who?"

She shrugged. "I dunno. Some jerk selling things."

"You mean you answered the door?"

"Sure. He rang and rang. I had to."

"I told you not to," he said, close to fury again. "What happened? What did he say?"

Jo-Anne giggled. "He said: 'Hallo, Mrs. Carter.' "

"*What?*"

"Oh, come on—he must have read it on the mail box. What's it matter, anyway? What are you so afraid of?"

"I'm not afraid of anything. I just don't have girls here, that's all."

"Scared of your wife?"

He let it go. "What happened with the man?"

"Oh, we talked it up a little. He was selling swimsuits." She giggled again. "He pulled out a bikini, and looked at me, and said: 'I guess I'm too late with this one.' He was kind of cute."

Carter stifled his sense of disgust. "Then what?"

"Then nothing. He went away again. He—"

"And that's what you're going to do," Carter broke in. "Here and now."

"I can't," she answered, rather more firmly than she had spoken before. "I told you, I feel lousy. I keep getting these pains."

"That's just too bad," he said harshly. "But it's your problem, not mine. You'll just have to go to a hospital, that's all. You can't have the baby here."

She answered very quietly: "Why not?" and with that, they were plunged headlong into bitter dispute.

It started as pleading on her part, blank denial on his; she must have spent most of the day thinking about this, getting her arguments ready, and he had a hard time stemming the flood. She *couldn't* go to a hospital, said Jo-Anne, with, for the first time, something like animation in her plain pudding of a face; she hadn't any money, they wouldn't take her in for nothing, she hadn't even got a nightgown. . . . And then, there was all the publicity; she'd have to give her name and everything, there would be all sorts of inquiries, maybe the police; how could she explain what had happened to her, what would the doctors say, they'd probably throw her out on her ear. . . . And she couldn't go back home, either; her parents wouldn't have her, and even if they did, it would be all over town, everyone would know, she couldn't stand everybody staring at her. . . .

"Don't you see," she said vehemently, "I want to keep this a secret! I don't want anyone else to know. You've *got* to help me."

The phrase was the very same one she had used at the beginning of all this, while they were still in his car; and, remembering it, Carter found himself reacting forcibly.

"How can you keep it a secret?" he asked, exasperated. "You need a doctor, nurses, everything. You can't have a baby in *secret*. It doesn't make sense!"

"I could, I could! I just need some help, that's all. I just need a place like this to stay."

"But how could you—" He paused; he did not even know the words, the right questions to ask. "I mean, I'm not a doctor, I wouldn't be any use. I don't know the first thing about it."

"I can fix it," she said stubbornly.

"What do *you* know about it?"

"Enough." Her eyes had turned aside, as if what she knew was not to be shared with anyone. "Two of my sisters had babies."

"I'll bet. . . ." But he was really beyond the wish to score easy points such as that one. "Good God, all sorts of things could go wrong. You might die!"

"I'm tough. . . . I'll die if you make me leave. That's for sure."

"That's ridiculous."

"It isn't! I won't have everyone knowing about this! I'd rather die!"

"Oh, for God's sake! . . . You said yourself, this happens to lots of girls."

"That's because you were acting so shocked. And I didn't really mean it, not the way I said. I don't feel so good about it. It's different when it happens to you."

He turned away from her, already grown sick of the futile argument. He wanted to enjoy his evening, he wanted to have a swim or catch a fish, he wanted to be alone and at peace again. This stupid idiot of a girl was spoiling everything. . . . Behind him, he heard her begin to speak again.

"There's some things I haven't told you," she said.

"I wouldn't doubt it."

"Don't be like that. . . . I—I've got a chance of marrying someone. Once all this is out of the way."

He turned and looked at her again, trying to guess

if she were lying or not. There wasn't much expression on the stolid face, but her hands, clenching and unclenching, seemed to be telling what her face did not—that she was becoming desperately anxious.

"Go on," he prompted. "Marrying who? The father?"

"No. Another guy. He's been away three or four months, construction work, up north somewhere. He can't have heard anything about this. When he comes back—" She paused. "I mean, if no one knew about the baby, it would be like a fresh start."

"Is that why you left town?"

"Yes."

"Didn't your folks kick you out?"

"No. They don't know about this either. They think I've got myself a job somewhere."

"Is your dad really a minister?"

"No," she answered again. "He works on the railroad."

"Well, my God!" said Carter, expelling a deep breath. "Why all the stories?"

"I thought—I wanted it to sound better than it was."

He could understand that, though he did not like it any the more for understanding it; rather the reverse—he was even less inclined to help someone who, from the very beginning, had tried to fool him

with such a string of lies. This girl really was a mess.
. . . He could see how desperation had been driving
her, if this latest story were true; and even if not, she
was still under pressure, she was still cornered, she
still had the baby which no one else could have, which
she would never really be rid of.

But it was her own fault, just the same; she should
have thought of all this earlier, before saying yes, or—
depending on truth or falsehood—before she had got
herself into a situation where she could not say no.
Why should he himself get involved—not only with
her, as had happened already, but in such a crazy
idea as trying to keep the birth a secret? She had no
right to ask it, and he would be a fool to let the thing
go any further.

He made his decision. "I'm sorry," he told her. "I
know you're in a tough spot, but I just can't help you.
It wouldn't work, and I don't want any part of it, anyway. You'll have to go."

"But why?" she insisted. Her hands were still
gripping and ungripping, as if she were actually wrestling with her troubles. "Why can't I stay? Who's
going to know about it? You look after yourself,
don't you?"

"Yes," he said. "But—"

"Then there won't be anyone nosing around, cleaning up. And if you have any friends calling, I can al-

ways stay in the bedroom. It can't be more than a week, after all." Once again, he could see that she must have been working on this throughout the day; she had all the answers, and they were beginning to add up. "There's just your wife, and she's away. Is she likely to come back?"

"No. Well, not without letting me know."

"There you are, then. We've got it made!"

He shook his head vigorously; the word "we" in her last sentence had struck a raw nerve, and an instinct of self-protection made him react immediately. There wasn't going to be any "we" about this situation. . . . But before he could answer, she had started the pressure again; and now her voice had lost its pleading tone, and was firming up towards something quite different, something with a threat in it.

"It's no good shaking your head, mister. You're in this thing already. What do you aim to do? Put me out? Do you really think I'll go, just like that?"

"You'll have to go."

"Try it, and see."

He frowned. "Then the police will take care of you."

"You want the police here? What are you going to tell them?"

"The truth. Just what happened."

"You try *that!* Don't forget, I'll be telling them

the truth, too." An unpleasant little smile played around the corners of her mouth. "Wait till you hear my story. Wait till they do."

"What story? This is all nonsense! What could you say? What could you prove?"

"Nothing, maybe. But I'll think of something good. Enough to get us into the newspapers. Enough to start people talking. You want to be in the newspapers? What about all your big-shot pals down at the town hall?"

She had found another nerve, and this time it was more tender still. What she had said could quite possibly come true; there wasn't any doubt that she could, and would, "think of something good," and it would not lose anything in the retelling. Whatever happened, there was certain to be talk, there was sure to be scandal; people would start thinking, and wondering, and digging; even if, as was bound to happen, Jo-Anne Broom were shown to be lying and his own version were believed, there would still be speculation, and gossip, and an endless round of dirty jokes.

The girls in the office would giggle and whisper, the town clerk would be forever looking down his nose, the mayor himself might have to answer questions in Council, and then start asking some of his own. . . . Carter knew he couldn't afford this—not

in his work, not in any other part of his life. . . .
He stepped away from her, and stood at the window,
facing the peaceful river. It was a beautiful evening,
calm and still; the sun, low on the horizon, cast a
bright gleam across the water; the boats drifting by,
the fishermen standing up to cast or lazily trolling,
were all part of the same picture of content.

This was where he belonged, this was what he
loved, and it was being threatened, it could be taken
away. What had happened, so suddenly, to the small
corner of the world he had carved out for himself?

Close behind him he heard her voice again, spiteful, determined:

"Better make your mind up."

"Shut up," he said, without turning. And then:
"I'm going for a swim. We'll settle this when I get
back."

*

4

The week that followed was a very curious one; it had been a long time since Carter had spent so many days and nights of furtive, concealed activity, or had been driven by such desire to escape the world's notice. Surprisingly, Jo-Anne made it easy for him; having won a crucial battle, she did not push her luck; she really seemed to be trying to repay him by doing what she was told—not answering the door or telephone, not appearing anywhere near a window, and of course never going out of the house.

He could not guess how she passed her time, though it was probably in doing absolutely nothing. But though she was making their concealment easy, she took no trouble to make it pleasant.

She had moved into his bedroom, while he spent his nights on the living room sofa; and from the bedroom there came, at any hour of the day or night, the endless thudding and twanging of the local radio station's "Top Sixty" hit parade, the cheeky young announcer's flip jokes, the raucous hard-sell commercials for soap and cars and farm machinery. Once, when he came home at lunchtime, he found her still asleep on his grimy, tumbled bed, and by her side the radio blaring out the same dreary rubbish. He had switched it off, and she had woken up suddenly and whined: "What's the matter with you? Leave it on!"

She was waiting, as he was waiting, for delivery; and she seemed to have even less idea of how to pass the time than he had.

No one bothered them, no one called—or, if they tried to make contact, they did not persist in face of the shut door, the apparently empty house. There were too many other things for river-side folk to do at this moment of the year; it was high summer, and people were making the most of it; the season of outdoors was ideal for insuring that intruders stayed at arm's length.

Carter's few friends seemed to accept the fact that, when the door was not answered, he had either gone fishing, or was asleep, or did not choose to be disturbed. Theirs was the sort of community which made allowances for all these things.

Jo-Anne Broom, of course, found fault with this isolation, whichever way it showed itself.

"You don't have many friends, do you?" she commented one evening, when he had got back from work and was busy setting the living room to rights. "You know, there hasn't been a single soul around, all day."

"Good," said Carter. "That's the way I want it."

"Is it? Don't you like people?"

"Not at the moment."

"Or don't they like you?"

He smiled; as usual, he did not feel inclined to argue. "That might be the answer."

"But don't you *mind?*"

"No. Why should I? It's the way I live. I like being alone. That's why I got this place on the river."

"What about your wife?"

"There's no argument there."

"Well, it seems funny to me. Back home, we had people around all the time."

"Maybe you should have stayed home."

She flared up. "You know I had to get out! What sort of an answer is that?"

But when things happened differently, when something else took the place of isolation, she was just as quick to complain about it.

"There was some woman hanging around the house this morning," she told him on another occasion. "She kept ringing and ringing the doorbell. She just wouldn't go away. She was here half an hour—I nearly went nuts!" Her eyes sharpened. "She wasn't your wife, was she?"

"What did she look like?" asked Carter.

"Sort of old. Grey hair. She had a dog with her."

"No," said Carter. "That's not my wife."

"Well, whoever it was, I wish she'd get lost. Honestly I could have walked right out and taken a swing at her, the way she wouldn't give up."

"Maybe she heard the radio going."

"Is that her business? She was staring in the window! What sort of people do you have around here, anyway?"

"They're just neighbours."

Jo-Anne sniffed, and pulled her dress across her ample front. "Neighbours, schnaybours! They're too damned nosy for me. God, will I be glad to get out of here!"

There were all sorts of answers to that, but Carter did not make any of them. Jo-Anne often talked like this; she was that sort of girl; he could not change her, any more than he could change the muddy colour of her eyes or the harsh fact of her pregnancy. All he could do was wait, and, while waiting, lead as solitary and self-contained a life as the situation allowed him.

He spent most of his evenings on the river, in the small twelve-foot outboard skiff which served him as his fishing platform; the mid-June sun gave him light till nearly nine o'clock, and he used the time for the sport he loved—fishing for pike and lake trout and bass, out in the stream where the shallow reed-lined river deepened and widened to make a slow-running, thirty-foot trench.

There were always a lot of other boats about, moving up and down or snugly anchored in a favourite spot; and Carter could identify many of the owners at a glance—by the shape of their craft, the size of their motors, the colour of their clothes. There were the old-timers, who knew every inch of their beat blindfold—the "river-rats," they called themselves, and seemed proud of the label. There were the tourists who came back year after year to this same guaranteed haven, and the kids who flogged the stream with an outsize lure for a few restless minutes, then roared away with all the authority of a seventy-five-

horsepower motor, impressing the fish much more
than their fellow-fishermen.

Carter would wave to some of these near-compan-
ions, and perhaps watch when a landing net was lowered and a prize scooped in, and then chug away up or
down stream in search of more quiet waters. At dusk
he would make for the shore, the ripples chattering
under the bow of his skiff, the cottage lights coming
on one by one, guiding him homewards; perhaps empty-handed, perhaps with something besides content-
ment to show for his time.

As he approached the dock, he would check to
make sure that Jo-Anne had not grown careless and
could be seen from the river; and then—if he had
been lucky—he would clean and cook his trophy,
and presently serve a strange, rather unreal supper for
two.

Jo-Anne took no part at all in this or any other
domestic routine; she was, in fact, absolutely useless
in anything which concerned housekeeping. She
could not cook, and seemed to be rather proud of the
fact. She had washed the dishes once, and broken two
plates and stopped up the sink with coffee grounds.
Smoking in bed, she burned a hole in a sheet; she always left the bathroom like a pigsty, she forgot to
flush the toilet. Lazy, bad-tempered, sluttish, she did
nothing but lie in bed, listen to the radio, or slop

around the house like a soiled and frowzy balloon.

It continually astonished Carter to think that this wretched human being had somehow attracted a man; that she had actually had an offer of marriage; that— married or not—this was a future mother of the race. . . . What it was going to be like when she had her baby, he could not begin to imagine. He had a mental picture of the child itself as a miniature version of Jo-Anne, and he recoiled from the prospect with a sharp revulsion.

Yet, for all this, on these lonely, shut-in, secret evenings, they were somehow drawn together; like people who, sharing certain criminal secrets, had no one else to talk to. With all doors locked, and all curtains pulled tightly together, they were boxed in, and they had to put up with it; it was inevitable that, however much they disliked each other, they contrived to grind out a certain minimum relationship, and somehow make it limp along to its appointed end.

When they talked, it was often a hopeless jumble of argument, disjointed comment, and (on her part) a jeering disagreement with all the rules, all ordinary opinion. Yet they did, at least, talk.

He found that he could still be sorry for her, in spite of what she was and what she did and said; just as he had felt sorry for her, that first evening when it all started, when he had seen her walking along the highway. It was this sense of pity which, one evening after work, made him make a detour of fifty miles to a town twice the size of Stampville, and there plod the streets till he found a cut-price store called "Hush-a-Bye Baby," and buy, with the shortest possible discussion, an all-in, inclusive, seventeen-dollar layette set, packaged in a cardboard carton labeled "Number One Son."

He had been nervous when he went in; by the time he came out, pursued by glances and giggles and an atmosphere of saccharine conspiracy, he was frankly sweating. But he had got what he wanted; and when he told Jo-Anne about it, and showed her his purchase, she actually thanked him, for the first time since she had set foot in the house.

"Well, gee!" she said. "Aren't you cute? . . ." She was digging deep into the box, bringing up handfuls of diapers, cotton vests, woollen bootees, bottles, a plastic pail, a card pierced with rubber nipples. She held up a knitted jacket, turning it this way and that as if it were something out of a museum. "Wild! . . . You wouldn't believe they were as small as this, would you?"

"They've got to start somewhere," said Carter, pleased with her show of interest.

"I know where they start," answered Jo-Anne smartly. But she really was, for a brief moment, almost normal, almost human, almost young again. "Thanks anyway, Jack. . . . I was just thinking we ought to get something—you know, to start it off."

She sat down on the sofa, and began to pack the things back into the box again, arranging and rearranging as if she were playing with toys. Carter stared at her with something like compassion. She was, as usual, looking terrible—ugly, puffy in face and body, an unrelenting slattern. The clean white diapers she was handling contrasted painfully with the soiled skirt and smock which had been her uniform ever since she arrived. He said, without thinking:

"I should have got something for you as well."

"Like a mink coat?"

He frowned. "I mean, something to wear around the house. . . . Look, why don't you go through the things in the closet, choose something you could use. A housecoat, something like that."

She shook her head, still intent on the baby's outfit. "I don't want to fool around with your wife's clothes."

"It wouldn't matter."

"Why? Isn't she coming back?"

After a pause, he answered: "No."

At that, she transferred her interest back to Carter.

"Well, what d'you know? . . . Now he tells me. . . . What happened?—did you have a row?"

"A lot of rows," he answered. He did not know why he was telling her this; it was the first time he had spoken of it to anyone. But Jo-Anne was the first person who had been there to listen. "She's been gone for over a year."

"But where is she?"

"Staying with her sister. Out in California somewhere. They live in a trailer, keep moving about. I don't know the address."

"Doesn't she write you, then?"

"No."

"And she's not coming back?"

"No."

"How long were you married?"

"Eight years, on and off." He felt the need to add to this. "But I told you, we had rows all the time. She left me a couple of times before, then she came back. But it was never any good. Nothing but quarrels. She—she used to throw things. She used to hit me."

"You should have hit her back," said Jo-Anne, with a certain authority.

Carter shook his head. "I don't like hitting people."

"But you know—just once."

"It's still wrong."

"Teach her a lesson." Jo-Anne considered. "Well,

as long as she's not coming back. . . . There's a bathrobe would just suit me. The one with the flowers on. D'you mind if I take it?"

"Help yourself," answered Carter. "It's just collecting dust, hanging there."

"That's what I thought."

She took to wearing the bathrobe, and then other clothes of his wife's—a nightgown, a kimono with a pattern of scarlet dragons. It gave Carter a very strange feeling to see her suddenly across the room, perhaps with her back towards him, dressed in clothes which he had not seen for more than a year, but which he remembered hating because he had hated the person inside them.

Indeed, it made him feel almost ill, the first time, and it did not help much to realize that the girl now inside them was, in her own way, also quarrelsome, and bad-tempered, and grudging, and perhaps would grow to rival his wife as the years passed. . . . But that was going to be someone else's problem. At the moment, Jo-Anne Broom, in her present version, was quite enough for him to cope with.

A full week passed, and then another day, and then, at noon on the second Saturday, while he was getting himself a leisurely meal and enjoying the break in routine, she suddenly called through from the bedroom:

"Hey! Can you hear me?"

Intent on what was in the frying pan, he answered: "Yes. What is it?"

There was a pause, as if she were busy with other things, and then she said, in a tightened kind of voice:

"I think it's on the way."

Carter had tried to make himself ready for this moment, but the cold chill, the near panic which now took hold of him, could not be resisted. He should never have agreed to this, he couldn't begin to cope with it, he just didn't know enough. . . . He turned off the stove, set down the frying pan, and walked through into the bedroom, slowly and fearfully, to meet whatever was in wait for him.

He had not really known what to expect, but he was relieved to see that, for the moment, things were normal enough. The room was the usual dirty shambles which he had come to associate with Jo-Anne; the contents of the "Number One Son" box were strewn on the floor around the bed, and the bed itself a rumpled mess which had not been made for three or four days. In the middle of this, the girl lay, framed in squalor, like a shapeless, overblown vegetable.

But there was pain in her face, and she had pulled up her legs in a rigid attitude of expectancy.

"What's happening?" he asked.

"What the hell do you think?" She drew in her

breath sharply, and held it for a long moment, and then let it go again. Her body relaxed. "That's better. . . . I guess this is the day."

His fear returned. "What—what do you want me to do? How long will it be?"

"How should I know? This can go on for hours. Just take it easy."

"All right." But he could not feel easy, nor ready to deal with whatever lay ahead; he wanted, more strongly than ever before, to escape from this trap before it was too late. "Look, let me call a doctor. Let him take over. It's stupid to do it this way."

She was staring back at him; he realized suddenly that she was tough enough to deal with him, and the baby as well. "No one's going to take over. . . . This is the way we're going to do it. You promised. Remember?"

"Yes, but—" he began. He was nearly distraught, and it showed in his face.

"Oh, don't be such a creep! People have babies all the time. It never stops. I can take care of it, easy."

"Are you sure?"

"Course I'm sure!" She grinned at him suddenly. "I've done it before."

"You mean, you've had another child?"

"Why not? I'm married."

He felt himself starting to get angry, in spite of all

his fear. This girl never ceased to make a fool of him, even on an occasion like this.

"But why didn't you say so? Why tell all those lies?"

"Well, you lied to me about your wife."

He began to straighten up the room, putting the baby's things back in the box, emptying ashtrays, smoothing rugs. He felt a little better now; maybe she *could* deal with this, as she had said.

"What happened?" he asked after a pause. "Where's your husband? Did he leave you?"

"Of course not! Why would he do a thing like that? . . . He's away somewhere. He's the one that's working on the construction job."

"But doesn't he know about this?"

She shook her head, irritatedly, as if Carter were being more stupid than a man had any right to be. "That's what it's all about. He's been away nearly a year. But he'll be back in a couple of months."

"So that's why you wanted it to be a secret."

"Sure. Why should I bother him?"

"But he's bound to find out."

"How?"

He did not answer, but went on with his tidying and straightening, glad to have something to do in a situation which was such a fantastic way out from normal. Now, it seemed, she was married, with a child fathered by somebody else, a child which had to be kept a secret, and somehow disposed of before her husband got back. . . . Carter had by now almost lost track of the different versions she had given him; perhaps this was another counterfeit card from the same pack of lies. . . . There was only one thing, out of all this, which must be true—he glanced at the gross, swollen body on the bed; she *was* pregnant, she *was* in his bed, she *was* going to have a baby, probably before the day was out.

As if to point up this fact, she suddenly wrenched herself sideways and away from him, overtaken by a fierce spasm of pain. He watched—he had to watch —as she dealt with it, and let it ride, and finally mastered it. He could well believe that she had had a child before. He wanted it to be true. . . . Finally she was quiet again, and brushed the damp yellow hair out of her eyes, and propped herself up on the pillows, and said perkily:

"Won't be long now, I guess."

"How long?"

"Some time tonight. . . . I told you, this can go on for hours. . . . Give me a cigarette, will you?"

He found one, and lit it, and passed it to her. She lay back, staring at the ceiling, blowing smoke upwards with deep draughts of breath. Amazingly, she was in charge of this situation, the calm centre of a storm more violent than any man could measure.

"I'd still like to call a doctor," Carter said hesitantly.

"Don't waste your money."

"Well, is there anything I can do?"

"Not a thing. Just relax, take it easy." She licked her lips unexpectedly, and her pale, pudgy face woke to life. "Tell you what—make me a fried egg sandwich."

*

5

Carter was never to forget that night; the most fright-
ening, crude, and disgusting night he had ever experi-
enced. Halfway through, he found a moment to pause,
and look at himself instead of her, and consider the
sort of activity he had been caught up in, the things
this damned girl was making him do. . . . He would
never have believed any of them possible; and if he had
known beforehand what the birth was going to en-
tail, he would not have hesitated to call an ambulance,

a doctor, a policeman, a neighbour—anything and anyone to get him out of an appalling ordeal.

Never mind the scandal, never mind the troubles that might come after; he could take them all, rather than another moment of this. . . . As he bent to continue his task, he found himself swearing that, as long as he lived, he would never get himself involved in anything which could bring him within five miles of this sort of scene.

Jo-Anne Broom was really very good—he had to admit that. She took charge, she told him what to do, she showed an element of fortitude he would never have guessed at. If this were the real girl, then she deserved a better deal in the future. . . . But that was only half the story, as far as he was concerned; however much the girl was able to do, he was still the doctor, and the clumsy midwife, and the hospital orderly who had to clean up the mess afterwards.

It was a boy, eventually; a tiny, puny, crumpled creature which emerged into the world scarlet, and then swiftly turned pale, and stayed that way, like a sickly slug. It cried all the time, on the same thin wail of complaint; it cried as Carter gave it separate life, cried when he sluiced it timidly in warm water, cried when he dried it and gave it back to Jo-Anne.

She looked exhausted to the point of death, but she

was wide awake, just as she had been all the time—wide awake to the battering waves of pain, to prolonged effort, to the brave self-control which had kept her from uttering a sound, all the way through.

She laid the baby in the crook of her arm, without a word, without a smile. Then, after a long time, she said: "It's alive," and shut her eyes as if she had already had enough of the holy estate of motherhood.

Carter did the rest of what he had to do, as quickly as possible; cleaning up, changing sheets and blankets, and presently burning all evidence of this new life—except the life itself—in the old-fashioned basement furnace. He felt so strung-up, and yet so tired, that he might have had the child himself; he walked to and fro, and up and down the steps to the basement, as if struggling towards the end of a nightmare.

Presently, at five o'clock in the morning, when Jo-Anne had said nothing more for a long time, and the grey-faced, shriveled newcomer only whimpered when it seemed to realize the sort of world it had been born into, Carter lay down on the sofa, still dressed, and turned his head away from the dawn light already pushing its way through the curtains, and fell into exhausted sleep.

He awoke to Sunday noontime, and the loud sound of the front doorbell. For a moment, in confusion, he could not even remember why the noise should give him such a swift stab of fear; and then the child cried from within the bedroom, and the real bad dream succeeded the false good one.

He looked about him uncertainly for a few seconds; then he crossed to the television set, and switched it on. When the sound was going full blast, he walked through and opened the front door.

It was only Danny Frost, but even Danny Frost was too much, at a moment like this.

"Hi, Jack!" said his next-door neighbour and fishing accomplice. He was a cheerful fat man who, during the week, sold coal and lumber; at the weekend, he gave up any pretense of enjoying this, and took to the river instead. "How about coming out for a try?"

"I can't, Danny," said Carter. "I've got things to do."

"Who hasn't?" Danny cocked his ear to the sound of the television, from which the music of a cartoon film was contributing a strident racket. "What's got into you, watching the kids' show?"

"I wasn't watching," answered Carter. He stood leaning against the doorpost, effectively blocking the view; on any other day of the year, he would have asked Danny in for a drink, and the knowledge made him ill at ease. "Sorry, Danny. The place is in a real mess. I'm taking the day to clean it up."

"So it's in a mess," said Danny Frost cheerfully.

"Leave it be. . . . Honest, Jack, I caught a muskie as big as that, just before dinner. Eight pounds, six ounces. . . . Let's go out again."

"I can't," said Carter again. "Some other time, eh?"

Danny looked at him suspiciously, and made a pretense of trying to peer behind him. "What's going on in there? Looks kind of dark to me. You shacked up, or something?"

"Just that," said Carter. He managed a grin, and started to shut the front door again, gradually, politely. "I knew you'd understand."

Danny shook his head. "Well, if I didn't know better. . . ." He turned, ready to go back to his car. "O.K.," he said. "Be a hero. But don't blame me if there aren't any fish left in the river."

"Enjoy yourself," Carter called after him.

"You enjoy yourself with Bugs Bunny," said Danny, "and whoever else you've got in there."

The rest of that day, and the rest of that night, were on the same pattern. He kept the curtains drawn, he cleaned up, he fetched and carried for Jo-Anne; he watched as she tried to nurse the child, and, when this proved inadequate, he brewed a mixture of warm milk and water which, between feeble wails, was sucked down slowly, a drop or two at a time, as if the child had lost interest in life from the moment it had found out what life was all about. It looked awful—

sticklike, almost glistening with pallor, weak as the last of a litter of mongrels. Its enormous eyes, clouded, sunken, rimmed with black, stared reproachfully at a world it might not have time to understand.

It cried nearly all the time.

Monday morning came too soon, for everyone in the house, and especially for Carter who, dead-tired and very nervous, should have been at work in his office by eight o'clock. Reluctantly, after a whole series of interruptions, calls for help, and necessary errands, he decided that he could not possibly make it; and it was just after eight o'clock when he telephoned to say that he would not be coming in.

The announcement was not popular, as a snarly voice at the other end of the telephone made clear. It was Blagdon, the man in charge of his office, his senior by many years, and his perpetual, nagging overseer.

"What d'you mean, you're not coming in today?" demanded Blagdon. "We've got a whole load of work —there's a meeting of board-of-control at four o'clock —those estimates have to be ready for them—you know that. What's the matter with you?"

"I've got a cold," answered Carter, and coughed forlornly to prove it. "I woke up feeling terrible. I just can't make it."

"You've got a hangover, more likely."

"It's not that at all," said Carter. "I told you, I've got a cold."

"What about the estimates?"

"It's all on my desk." Carter knew that he had picked the wrong day to be away, and that he could not afford to attract this sort of attention; but he had no choice—there was too much to take care of at home, he had to guard this position also. . . . "The figures are in the green folder. It's all straightforward. . . . I'm sorry," he said again, conscious of many kinds of danger. "I just feel lousy. I wouldn't be any good, anyway."

"You're damned right, you wouldn't be any good," said Blagdon sharply. "That seems to be your motto these days." This was quite untrue, and they both knew it, but Blagdon was not the man to miss the chance of using the knife, if the weapon came his way. "Well, if you're not coming in, you're not coming in. I'll mark you up for one day's sick leave. Right?"

"Whatever you say."

"It's not what I *say*," said Blagdon, in the same sharp, nagging tone. "It's what's in the book. . . . And let me tell you, you certainly picked a hell of a day to fall down on your job."

"I can't help it. The way I feel, I've just got to stay home."

"I'd like to stay home myself," said Blagdon. "Specially on a Monday morning. Who wouldn't? . . . Well, you'd better get back to bed. Lie down before you fall down. O.K.?"

Carter was both angry and afraid when he put down the phone. Blagdon could do him a lot of harm at the town hall; he was a spiteful gossip as well as a rough taskmaster; this story, with plenty of embroidery, would certainly reach the personnel manager, and it might even reach the mayor. . . . His anger, in full measure, went out to Jo-Anne Broom, who had not only worked him into an appalling position, but might actually be putting his job in danger. Carter was far from having enough seniority, or security, to risk black marks, departmental jokes, a Monday morning reputation for weekend wildness.

The list of things he could not afford to have happen to him was growing longer by the hour, and this girl was the author of every one of them.

But there was worse to come that day; and, at its end, the worst thing of all.

Carter was enjoying a spell of doing nothing when the visitor took him by surprise. He had been working all morning; he had prepared bottles for the baby, and done some laundry, and cooked lunch for Jo-Anne, who said she felt much better and was going to try getting up. After lunch, Carter went to the front door, more to feel the sun on his face than anything else; and just as he opened the door, the stranger mounted the top step and stood before him.

He was a small, hungry-looking man, thin, sharp-featured, with a professional kind of cheerfulness which could not have been more than skin-deep. He was carrying a shabby, bulging suitcase, and, as Carter faced him, he set it down with an exaggerated sigh of relief, and said:

"Hi there! You must be the man of the house."

There was no chance to avoid him; to close the door again would have been impossible, and for Carter to draw it shut behind him would have seemed too suspicious altogether. He was caught, and he knew it. Praying for all sorts of things, and principally that the baby might keep quiet, he answered, as curtly as he could:

"What do you want?"

It was rough, and totally discouraging, but it must have been the sort of thing this man was used to. He smiled, broadly and falsely, and held out his hand, which Carter had to take, and answered:

"I'm Joe Pepper. Is Mrs. Carter in?"

"No," said Carter. "That is—" His glance fell onto the suitcase, and from it he took the only clue available. "Are you selling something?"

"Sure I'm selling something!" said Joe Pepper, with

great heartiness. "I'm selling whatever the ladies want
—and that's usually plenty! Ain't it the truth? I was
here awhile back, and Mrs. Carter said—"

"She's not in," said Carter.

"Oh." The other man's face dropped, and then, as
quickly, regained its brisk optimism. "She's gone into
hospital, eh?"

Carter found himself growing cold, in spite of the
warm afternoon sunshine. This thing was getting too
involved, too close to him altogether. Before long, the
whole world would be sharing his secret, and would
then move in and do something about it. He tried to
fend this off, as best he could.

"What are you talking about?"

"Well, you know. . . ." Joe Pepper was now looking at him in a way which Carter did not like at all; as
if they belonged to the same all-male, locker-room
confederacy, knowing the score, sharing the joke, admitting that these things just did happen. . . . "I
brung some stuff for the kid, like she said. How about
taking a look?"

"No," said Carter. "There's no—"

His denial froze on his tongue just in time, as, from
behind him, there came the sharp, unmistakable sound
of the child crying.

Joe Pepper's face sprang into new and spurious life.

"Well, *well!*" he said, smiling broadly. "Why all the big secret?" He held out his hand again. "And where's my cigar, for gosh sakes? Was it a boy or a girl?"

Something inside Carter seemed to give way suddenly. He felt that if this went on for a moment longer, he would do something fantastic, something fatal—start shouting, or take a swing at the grinning nuisance in front of him. He could not bear to hear a single further question from the outside world. He said loudly:

"Mind your own business!"

The other man lost his smile, and his face sharpened into sudden wariness. But he was jaunty still, in spite of the rebuff; apparently there was nothing he had not heard on doorsteps, nor any new surprises in the selling game.

"O.K., O.K. . . . Sorry I spoke. . . . How about taking a look—"

"No!" shouted Carter. "I don't want anything! Take the damned stuff away!"

"Well!" said Joe Pepper, on a very unpleasant note. "I certainly hit *you* on the wrong day, didn't I? I'm just trying to make a buck, you know. There's no law against it."

"Make it somewhere else."

"That'll be a real pleasure," said Joe Pepper, and

started to laugh in his face. As Carter slammed the door shut, he heard his caller still laughing on the other side of it, with a harsh, insistent mockery which was his first offering of the truth.

Carter leaned back against the door, breathing hard, shaken beyond endurance by anger and fear. All the things he was desperately scared of seemed to be happening, in their own fatal sequence; he was drawing attention to himself, he had earned a black mark at the office, and now a third person knew that there was a child in the house. And it was all due to this worthless girl, a girl to whom he owed nothing, a girl he didn't even like as a human being. . . . He nearly lost control of himself as he heard her voice, coming from the bedroom above the whining of the child:

"What was all that about?"

After a moment, when he had done his best to collect himself, he walked through, and looked at Jo-Anne. She was in his bed, as usual, enthroned on the grimy pillows like some ugly souvenir of love; the gaunt child lay by her side, its waxen face contorting as it forced out its feeble cries. And it was for this disgusting bed-full that he was running into danger. . . . He answered her roughly:

"It was that salesman again. He had some kid's clothes. Did you really ask him to come back?"

"I might have." She was unconcerned; she did not really care about anything, now that she was installed and immovable. "He said he'd be around."

"You must be mad!" Carter said furiously. "What did you do that for? You know we don't want people coming around here."

"He's a salesman," she answered indifferently. "You can't stop them."

"You *can* stop them! Just don't have anything to do with them, that's how to stop them. Did he say where he was from?"

"Not that I know of. Does *that* matter?"

"Of course it matters! Good God, if he's from Stampville—don't you see, I'm getting in a hell of a mess over this! He heard the baby crying, he knows that it's here. If he mentions it to anyone in Stampville, people will start asking all sorts of questions."

"It's not my fault," said Jo-Anne.

"Of course it's your fault!"

"I mean, it's not my fault the kid cries. I don't want people to talk, either." She looked down at the child, which was moving its spindly legs a bare inch at a time, and whimpering endlessly. "We've got to keep it quiet. Can't you give it a pill, or something?"

"I haven't got any pills."

"Well, aspirin."

"You don't give aspirin to babies."

"Oh yes, you do! I've seen it on TV. They make little ones specially. You know, the woman says, 'That's the dosage recommended for children,' and everyone's smiling all over. You must have seen it."

It was a temptation to believe this nonsense, and to act on it, but Carter could not bring himself to do so.

"That's for older children," he told her. "Babies aren't strong enough."

"This one's strong enough," she answered viciously. "Never stops yelling." She glanced down at it again, frowning, thoughtful. "All right, no aspirin. But if it cries much more, we've got to do something."

It did cry much more, whatever they tried; whether they changed it, or fed it, or rocked and soothed it, or left it alone. The nagging sound, muffled or not, now seemed to be built into the house; and to contain it there, which was now vital, they were forced to keep all the windows shut, and have the television turned up loud, on a stifling hot afternoon which itself cried out for peace, quiet, and a cool breeze from the river.

By evening, their nerves and tempers were all but in rags. Only the baby, never relenting, never distracted, kept to its own steady course.

Jo-Anne got up, at about nine that night, perhaps to try out her strength, perhaps to escape the noise which was closest to her; Carter felt her moving about, and then she came into the living room, slamming the bedroom door behind her with sudden violence.

He was reading a three-day-old newspaper, his back to the pounding television set. He looked up. He almost had to shout to be heard.

"How do you feel?"

"Like a dog."

She looked like a dog, too—a dog no one in his right mind would want to love, or feed, or own. She was thin now, like the baby, and almost as pale; her tattered curtain of hair framed a face which lacked any feature save a grim petulance. He said, as mildly as he could manage:

"Well, don't do too much."

"Don't you worry! I can't do *anything*." In a pause on the sound track of the TV program, the baby could be heard, wailing from behind the closed door. Jo-Anne said again: "We've got to do something about that," and fell into silent, sullen thought.

Presently she said: "I guess that's all for me," and went back into the bedroom.

*

6

Carter woke with a start about midnight, for no reason, and wondered instantly, fearfully, what had broken into his sleep. There must have been some sort of noise. . . . He sat up on the sofa, stretching out his cramped legs, and waited, listening. There was nothing to be heard; no noise from the bedroom, no crying from the child. Could it have been the silence which had woken him? He had fallen asleep to the sound of the baby still wailing; perhaps it had just stopped, and the change had reached some deadened nerve, and pulled him from sleep.

Then he noticed a line of light under the bedroom door. He was not the only one awake. He stood up, stretching again, and as he did so the door opened and Jo-Anne came out. Carter's guess about what had woken him up was now proved right, to a very terrible degree, as she said, in a voice not more lively than usual:

"I guess it's dead."

Some part of him had always been fearing this, but it was still a vile shock. "For God's sake!" he answered, nearly in panic. "What's happened?"

"Nothing."

"It can't be *nothing*."

"Maybe I rolled over on it, or something."

"Are you sure?"

"Sure I'm sure. Take a look."

He did not want to take a look; he wanted to run away, or put the clock back to his childhood, or wake up to find this was only a dream. But the bedroom door was open, and from within the bedroom, not a sound. He walked in, with dragging steps, to see what was there.

The child lay at the edge of the bed, its eyes and mouth open, yet completely still. As Carter drew near, and bent over it, it seemed to be staring back at him, with eyes curiously prominent; but there was no life in that stare—it was fixed forever, like all the rest, as blind and lifeless as the stare of any doll or puppet, of any lost child.

There was an intruding air of death here, which none of the living could deny, even if they had wanted to; which no tears could change, even if there had been tears to flow. Hesitantly, Carter stretched out his hand to touch the white face. There was a small warmth remaining, but nothing else, only sadness and stillness, and the mortal gulf between a man moving and a child immovable.

But there was one other thing present, and that was danger; and he woke instantly to this as soon as he came back to Jo-Anne.

She had switched on the light, and was standing by the fireplace, in his wife's scarlet kimono. He had not noticed this before, in the semidarkness; now the bright colour flared out at him, adding to his sense of distress and peril. Deeper and deeper was she pulling him in. . . . Fears which he hated, suspicions which he could not control, swirled round and round inside his head, looking for release. He asked her, in a low voice:

"What did happen?"

Apparently she did not see any need to whisper; she was not feeling the same as he; she was in much better shape altogether. "I told you, nothing happened," she answered readily. "I just woke up, that's all. I couldn't hear anything, so I switched on the light, and the kid wasn't breathing at all. It was out cold. What could I do? I waited a bit, then I called you."

"Why did you say you might have rolled over on it?"

"I read it somewhere."

It was a curious answer; he could not help wondering, with a sick feeling of doubt, if she had remembered "reading it somewhere" before or after she did it. . . . He tried to put the thought away, but it persisted.

"Surely you'd know if that was what happened."

"Not if I was asleep." She was lighting a cigarette, and she drew several satisfying breaths before she spoke again. "Like I said, that's what *might* have happened. Or it just died. Or it had a fit or something, with all that crying." She expelled another full waft of smoke, which lingered in the space between them. "It wouldn't have been much good anyway, would it?"

"What do you mean, 'anyway'?"

"I mean, if it ever grew up. Have you ever seen such a miserable little—" She broke off abruptly. "Oh, what's it matter?" she went on after a moment. "It was alive, now it's dead. Now you see it, now you don't. That's what you wanted, isn't it?"

"Of course I didn't want it to die!"

"It didn't sound that way to me. You were always going on about it crying. . . . What's it matter, anyway?" she asked again. She stretched her arms above her head; the loose sleeves of the kimono spread like scarlet wings. "It's all finished, and I'm free again."

"Free" was another word with several tormenting strings attached, a word which could only feed his fear and doubt. How could she feel free, unless this freedom were something she had longed for, perhaps worked for? How could she feel free, when this was only the beginning?

They were not free, any more than a man shackled to a length of chain was free; of course such a man could move, but he could not hide his dragging anchor, nor escape it. They had had a live child in the house, now they had a dead one. They were not free of the child, just because it was dead. In fact, they were now doubly shackled, first by its birth, now by its death.

He tried to establish this, to reach some part of her mind which might match his.

"We've got to report this," he told her. "Get it all cleared away. Then you can talk about being free."

"Report it? Who to?"

"The authorities."

"Well, you work at the town hall. Can't you fix it?"

"They don't fix things like this at the town hall. In fact, they don't fix anything at the town hall. It isn't that sort of place. . . ." She really had some crazy ideas, and some horrible ones. "This is something for the police."

He had caught her attention with the one important word, and she reacted briskly. "How do the police come in?"

"It's their job. Or the coroner's, anyway. There are all sorts of formalities. When someone dies, people have to know about it."

"Why?"

"Good God!" he exploded. "Don't be such an idiot! Because it's a death, that's why."

"I wouldn't call me an idiot, if I was you. . . . It's you that's the idiot. Telling the police means we have to explain everything."

"It means *you* have to explain everything."

There was a pause, while they stared at each other. Then she answered: "You know I can't do that."

"You have to."

"And you can't do it, either. I told you way back, you're in this thing already. And that was before the kid was even born. Now you really are in it." Suddenly she seemed to be examining him as if he were a very strange type of person, never met before, difficult to classify except as a freak. "I don't get it," she said. "Do you *want* to tell them what's been going on here, explain it to all the newspapers?"

"I'll explain what I have to. Don't you see?—there isn't any choice."

"There *is* a choice! My God, you better wake up and smell the coffee! You'll have enough trouble telling about picking me up, and the baby being born here, without a doctor. But now—" she smiled a crooked smile "—now you really have something to explain."

"Only that it died."

"You think that'll make everybody happy again?"

Now it was his turn to take a fresh look at Jo-Anne Broom. It was as if she were growing up before his eyes—growing up to confidence, to new authority, to a triumphant toughness which had ended her forlorn losing streak. Amazingly, she really had become free when the child died; she was freer than he was, because she did not give a damn about anything; she had managed to involve him more and more, while not losing any ground herself.

If it ever came to a wrestling match for public favour, she would get the verdict; she would be the

one to be believed, she would walk off with the sym-
pathy, while he was left with the guilty look and the
cries of "Foul!"

He could not quite see how she had done this, except that she was female, with more time and talent
for this sort of play. But at the moment he could not
even try to work it out; it was the middle of the night,
he was desperately tired and worried, yet somehow
he had to get up and go to work, within a few hours.
And there was still the dead child in the next room to
be taken care of. . . . More to give himself time to
think than anything else, he asked:

"What's the choice? What *can* we do?"

The answer was prompt and, in the circumstances,
brutal. "Get rid of it."

If he had had any sense at all, thought Carter, he
would have stopped right there. But this moment
didn't have any sense in it; he was going through the
peak of the nightmare, where people said and did
things which only afterwards one knew to be beyond
the limits of behaviour. Thus it was without surprise that he heard himself ask:

"How do you get rid of a dead child?"

"Easy," said Jo-Anne, as promptly as before. "People are doing it all the time. You ought to hear some
of the stories *I've* heard. . . . You can leave it somewhere, like in a locker at the bus station. You can

drive out into the country, and just—" she gestured "—just throw it away. I knew a girl once who put hers under a big Christmas tree on the shopping plaza. But she was caught—some bastard tried to steal it while she was still around. . . . Or you can bury it, if you've got a garden. Or there's the river. That's not too far away, is it?" She was looking at him with bright invitation, as if showing him around a favourite picnic spot; it was the first time he had seen her really interested in anything. "You can leave it in a motel, though you've got to watch out if they get the number of your car. You can just *mail* it to someone— you know, a false address. You can sink it in one of those things they catch lobsters in. You can build yourself a nice new cement walk. Honest, it's *no trouble!*" She had not finished, even now. "There was another girl I heard about, her boyfriend bought one of those electric carving knives—"

"Shut up!" Carter almost screamed at her. "God, you must be out of your mind! How can you even think of things like that?"

"I'm only trying to help."

"You're just disgusting!" A feeling of nausea, and another, quite different feeling, that if he went any further with this he would be ruined, swept over him; it was as much as he could do to speak another word to her. "Now you listen to me. We're not going to do anything like—like what you said. It's impossible. We wouldn't get away with it, not in a hundred years!"

"No harm in trying," said Jo-Anne.

"There's every harm. . . . Tomorrow morning, we're going to report all this. Everything that's happened, everything. You understand?"

"I think that's stupid," she said.

"Never mind what you think. That's how it's going to be." Suddenly he was overwhelmingly tired; if he did not get some sleep, here and now, he would drop where he stood. "I don't want to talk about it anymore. I'm going to bed."

"You know, you're being a damned fool."

"I've been a damned fool long enough."

She shrugged, and turned away from him; she was, it seemed, prepared to give up. "O.K. Have it your own way." Then she pointed towards the bedroom door. "Am I supposed to sleep in there?"

"I don't mind what you do."

He switched out the light, and moved back to the sofa, and lay down again. He was unspeakably weary; his eyes closed almost immediately, cutting off the fearful world. Presently he heard her going into the bedroom, and the door shutting. When, a few moments later, his eyes half-opened again, he saw that her light was still on. But he could hear nothing, nothing at all.

For a moment he wondered, in drowsy distaste, what she had done with—it; and then his brain refused to think any more about anything. Thankfully, weakly, he left all questions until the morning; and in the morning, she was gone.

7

*

"There's one thing sure," said Blagdon disagreeably. "If you make any more mistakes like that one, you'll end up in jail."

Carter passed his hand over his forehead, as unobtrusively as he could. His headache persisted, but he knew it would be a great mistake to admit the fact. Blagdon would certainly jump on it; it would only lead to more needling, more of this sort of thing.

"I'm sorry, sir," he said. The "sir" was unusual, but

he threw it in as an extra, a sop to his tormentor. "I guess I wasn't thinking."

"You guessed right," Blagdon snapped back. His bushy eyebrows, suspended like a dropped fringe between the bald head and the jowly chin, creased into a ferocious frown. "In fact, you must have guessed this whole damn' mess. Can't you even add up straight? What's the matter with you?"

"I'm sorry," Carter said again. There was really no way to appease this monster, this toad behind the desk; he could only take what was coming to him, and make his escape as soon as he could. "It must be this cold. I still don't feel too well."

"If you want to tie one on," said Blagdon, "then tie one on. But don't bring it back to the office."

"Honestly, it's not that at all. I had one of these colds last year. Remember? I stayed home then."

"You should have stayed home today. Then we wouldn't have this sort of mix-up."

Carter would indeed have given a lot of money— all his money—to have stayed home that day; it might not have solved any problems, but at least it would have given him a chance to catch his breath, after that morning's appalling surprise, and take stock of the terrors which were now pushing in on him from every side.

He had overslept, after a wretched night; he had woken with the headache hammering away at his temples, and seen, from a panic-stricken glance at the clock, that he had a bare twenty minutes to be dressed, and in his car, and on the road; and then, as he moved about in a nervous frenzy of speed, shaving like a shaking drunkard, dressing anyhow, feeling like a rag, knowing that he should have got up hours earlier to deal with yesterday's inheritance—then he had discovered that the house, except for himself, was empty.

Except for himself. . . . He would have given all the money over again, and half his expectation of life, if that had been true. It was a fact that Jo-Anne Broom was not in the house; it was a fact that the baby was no longer on the bed. For a moment, looking around the deserted bedroom, Carter had had a wild hope that for some reason she had relented; that, in disappearing, she had taken the child with her as well; and then he had noticed, not too prominently displayed near the window, the box labeled "Number One Son," and he had lifted its lid, with a sick foreboding, and found that the label on the box was now literally true.

He had slammed it shut again, and after it the bedroom door, and then the front door, tearing away from the loathsome scene, making his escape before his legs gave out, and his brain as well. Halfway to Stamp-

ville, he knew that he should have stayed home somehow—making any excuses, taking any chances with
the future. But he was cornered; he could not possibly miss another day at work, and perhaps he could
not have gone back to the house either, at that moment.

So he had followed routine. But routine could only
be a brief pause, like a break in a horror movie. It was
to the house and its terrors that he had to go back,
when this awful day at the office somehow came to an
end.

This awful day included, at the top of its list,
Blagdon himself, a cat-and-mouse artist who had still
not finished with him, who was still making the most
of a situation exactly suited to his talents.

"I just can't understand it," said Blagdon, as if he
had made a sincere and honest effort to do so, and had
been tripped up by the incomprehensible. "You've
made these schedules out a hundred times before. Now
suddenly they're all back-to-front. If I hadn't noticed
it—" He sighed and shook his head, in grief and
shame; his fat, flabby body in the creased alpaca jacket
might have been the only thing standing between Carter and public degradation in the market square. "You
know," he said, "if you don't smarten up, there's going to be some changes around here."

"I'm sorry," said Carter. He had now lost count of

the number of times he had said it; but he would keep on repeating his plea, if keeping on would somehow get the scene over, and the day disposed of.

"That makes both of us," said Blagdon snappishly. "Maybe you need *two* days at home to get over your weekends. . . . You must have been on moonshine. . . . Messing up the property schedules. . . ." He jabbed a pudgy thumb downwards at the offending papers. "Do these all over. . . . *That* goes *there*, and *that* goes *there*, and *that* goes *there!* And—" the thumb suddenly swept upwards through an arc in the air, and ended by pointing at the open window behind him "—if this sort of thing happens again, *you* go *there*."

Carter escaped, thankfully, and ground his way in and out of the maze of figures again, and somehow got through the rest of the day without attracting any more attention. As soon as he could, which was sixty seconds after Blagdon had stumped his way out of the office, Carter himself left the town hall, and got into his car, airless and oven-hot after a day parked in the sun.

He drove as quickly as he could through the traffic, and quickly out onto the highway; only as he neared home was he brought to understand what this pressure was doing to him, when his attention wandered, and he nearly went into the ditch, and his car came to a shuddering halt on the grass edge.

It was half past five when he reached the safety of the house. But this idea of safety took on an atrocious mockery as he shut and locked the front door behind him, and realized fully what he now had to face.

He faced it, first, as a coward; wandering slowly about the silent, darkened house, taking stock, delaying as long as he could the close examination of what he *must* see. . . . Jo-Anne Broom had not left empty-handed; there was a small suitcase missing, and some of his wife's clothes, and a few dollars—five or six—which had been lying in a desk drawer. The girl was a little better equipped now than when she had first arrived; but, in another sense, she was a thousand times more ready to face the world. She had shed her monstrous burden, and left it all to him.

This burden, he now had to meet, in the dreadful flesh.

When, for the second time, Carter lifted the lid of the box labeled "Number One Son," it was an even worse ordeal than the first discovery. The fact that he knew what he would find seemed to be pulling his hand back; the fact that his hand was trembling made him afraid that he might actually faint when the lid was lifted.

He did not faint, but he found himself looking with real horror at the tiny body, ivory-white, glazed in death; a shrunken wax doll which was the most lifelike toy he had ever seen. It was strange that so pitiful an object should be so terrifying, could make him shake and sweat; but he could not deny this power, which seemed to be turning him into an infant himself.

It was not the first dead body he had seen; yet in this poor, meagre, and neglected corpse he read a message so potent that it was all he could do not to give way entirely.

He was about to close the lid again when he noticed something new. There had been a crucial change since that morning—or perhaps it was only because he was now looking more carefully. Under the small dropped chin was something which he had taken to be a shadow, but which he now saw was a patch of discolouration; and as he bent closer, he found that it was more than a patch—it went, so far as he could see, all the way around the neck, in a wide livid band; it was a bruise in the form of a collar.

There might be some doubt of what had caused it, whether a scarf, a handkerchief, or a pair of human hands, but there could be no question of who and why; and with this, one last terror had been added to the total which now threatened to swamp his life.

No wonder Jo-Anne Broom had left secretly, by night. . . . He put back the lid of the box, more gently this time, and left the bedroom, almost tiptoeing in a sudden access of fear. There was guilt here, of a most grisly kind; and it was guilt which was shared, or would seem to be shared, by himself, the sole survivor of this never-to-be-explained triangle. He understood now, overwhelmingly, that he could not possibly report what had happened.

Jo-Anne had told him this, many times; and now she had clinched it.

He sat down on the sofa, and took off his spectacles, and dropped his head in his hands; but there was no comfort in this false solitude. There seemed to be two enormous enemies standing over him, ready to strike; one was people, the other was the law.

Blagdon stood for the people; Blagdon, and others like him—the gossipers in town, the loose-talkers on the local radio, the headline writers who could give him a sarcastic public label ("INNOCENT VICTIM," SAYS CARTER), or an all-but-libellous one (SLAIN CHILD: CARTER BLAMES "ABSENT" GIRL FRIEND), or tag him with a quotable joke (CARTER LEFT HOLDING THE BABY), and make it impossible for him to keep his job, or even to live in the district.

There would be scandal, there would be talk for years to come; in the country, they liked to chew such morsels very slowly, and there was enough here to keep them chewing for years. He would be in the very centre of the limelight, the thing he most feared and most hated; he would be forever the man who picked up that girl, and she had the baby, and it died, and they never found out who did it.

All this, even if he were found legally innocent. . . . Here the law stepped in, and here he was, in many ways, at the law's mercy. How could he explain the chain of involvement, to a sour-faced policeman who didn't understand that these things just happened, perhaps to a judge who felt like taking a stern line with loose operators like himself?

He had brought home a road-side pickup, a girl half his age: why? He had kept her for the night, and after that for many nights: why? He had concealed a birth: why? He had harboured a dead child: why? He had waited, at least a day, before reporting what looked very like a murder: why, why, why?

Somewhere along this fatal line, he would be trapped. They would never leave him alone, they would never leave the house alone. . . . *He had to do something*. What was that awful phrase that Jo-Anne Broom had used? "Wake up and smell the coffee." At last he had smelled the coffee, and caught a true whiff of its brew. Unless he slammed the lid on tight—

The doorbell rang.

Carter jerked his head up, instantly alert and afraid. The sound fitted in so well with what he had been thinking that it might have been these same thoughts coming true; he had been daydreaming of arrest, and now here were the police to arrest him. . . . He waited, listening, scarcely daring to move, while all around him the silent house seemed to be shouting out that something was wrong here, that a visitor need only step inside to find a murdered child and a guilty man. . . . He continued to wait, hoping that he could somehow keep his presence secret, even though his car was standing in the driveway; but then the bell rang again, in a particular way, and he was able to relax a little.

Whatever it was, it was not a policeman's ring; his caller was using that seven-note signal—ting-ti-ti-ting ting, *ting ting*—which children playing, and young men calling for their girl friends, and drivers impatient in a traffic jam, sometimes used to attract attention. The police were way above such childish tricks. . . . He got up, though it took some determination to do so, and walked into the hallway, and unlocked the front door, braced for whatever he might have to meet.

But when he opened it, it was to a friend; his fishing pal, Danny Frost.

Danny was grinning cheerfully, sure of his welcome. "What's going on?" he demanded in a loud voice. "You locking me out, or something?"

Carter forced an answering smile. "Sorry, Danny. I must have done it by mistake." He waited for a moment, wondering what to do next; and then he suddenly knew that he could not, for the second time, fail to invite Danny inside. It wouldn't make sense, it was too far out of line. He said, as normally as he could: "How about a drink?"

"You talked me into it," answered Danny Frost, and marched through into the sitting room.

Danny was dressed for fishing, as usual, in faded khaki slacks, plaid shirt, and a battered hat—which he kept on—with half-a-dozen gaudy-coloured trout flies stuck into the crown; he looked, Carter thought enviously, like a really free spirit. . . . When he had been handed his drink, he took a quick swallow, and then turned to stare out of the front window. The river was all that really drew him; the wide placid river with the fish rising, the boats going by, the evening sun slanting.

"Sure looks good tonight," he said happily. "How about it? You coming out?"

"I can't tonight, Danny," answered Carter.

Still staring at the river, Danny said: "Oh, come on,

Jack. It'll do you good. What's the matter? You don't like fishing anymore?"

"It's not that. I want to wash my car."

"Don't do it," said Danny, in mock alarm. "You might rinse it right down the drain." He turned, smiling. "Why don't you get yourself a new one? That old heap is just about ripe for the junkyard."

"I can't afford new cars. Not on my salary."

"Salary!" Danny snorted. "The sort of taxes I pay, you people at the town hall must all be millionaires. . . ." He took another gulp of his drink. "What's this about you having a baby in the house?"

Danny Frost had his back to the light, and Carter was directly facing it; it was a merciless exposure. Carter did his best, but he knew that his expression must have changed in a way which could have astonished the most stupid man, the slowest child, the dullest observer; and Danny Frost was none of these things. . . . He felt himself grow pale, and then scarlet; he raised his glass to his lips, but that could only cover half his face, leaving his frantic eyes to give the game away. Finally he managed to say:

"What are you talking about?"

"I thought you'd tell *me*," answered Danny, in his normal voice. He could not have been watching at all closely, or perhaps his mind had been still on the river and the fish; whichever it was, he did not seem to be finding Carter's expression anything out of the ordinary. "It's some story that Marge picked up. There was this guy selling clothes or something, door-to-door, and they got to talking, and he said there was a girl here. He said it was your wife, but I know better than that. He said there was a baby too."

Carter had only one choice, at that awful moment; a flat denial. Whatever else came after could only be dealt with, section by section, as it happened; it wasn't even any good guessing.

"Well, there wasn't," he snapped. "Whoever said that was just plain nuts."

"That's what I told her," answered Danny, secure in the world of male commonsense. "I said he must have the houses mixed up. Or else Marge got the story wrong. You know Marge—if she can get things back-to-front, that's where she'll get 'em. Women! . . . I love my wife," he said, on a cheerfully sarcastic note. "But she does get things mixed up."

Carter decided on an even bolder stroke. "That must have been Joe Pepper."

"Who's Joe Pepper, for God's sake?"

"Some jerk of a salesman." He remembered that this had been Jo-Anne Broom's own expression, and he hurried on from it. "He was around here bothering me, last week. Just wouldn't give up. I had to push him out, in the end. Maybe this was his idea of a joke. Spreading the word. You know, to get his own back."

"Funny way to go about it." But Danny seemed to be accepting it, as he did most other things, without much curiosity. "So I can tell Marge, you haven't had a baby?"

"No."

"Or a girl?"

"Or a girl either."

"It didn't sound like you," confided Danny. "But you never know, these days. Marge will be pleased, anyway. She thinks you're a solid citizen. Big contrast with me." He swallowed the last of his drink, and set the glass down on the nearest table. "Well, that's it. Thanks for the lifesaver. . . . Sure you won't come out?"

"I can't, Danny. It's a bit too late."

Danny glanced at his watch. "Only just after six. We'd have a good two hours before the light goes."

"Honestly, I can't."

"O.K."

He was preparing to take his leave, without, it seemed, any harm done at all. In his relief, Carter had an overwhelming impulse to tell him all his troubles; to shed some of the intolerable load onto this long-time, solid, cheerful friend, who might somehow think of a way to help him. But he knew that this was not possible; if there were a way, he would have to find it by himself, in secret, because friends, however solid and cheerful, could never actually share the fact of murder.

Friendship must always stop short, several comfortable yards on this side of the law. If he did tell Danny, Danny would first be astonished, and then sympathetic; he might even think up some plan of escape. But soon, very soon, he would begin to look thoughtful, and start talking about the police, and finally—whether by agreement or not—he would start talking *to* them.

Carter was now edging the other man towards the front door, without too much pushing, though he was in a fever to shut and lock it again. They stood chatting for a moment longer; and then Danny said, by way of good-bye: "Well, don't have a baby without telling me. You hear? It's not neighbourly!" and bounced his way out of the house.

Carter stood trembling on the other side of the door, until the noise of the foot-falls on the gravel faded. At last he had another breathing space. But now, he thought, alone in the silent house, still shaking uncontrollably—now he really *must* do something.

*

8

It took a long time to get the furnace going properly; much longer than on the night the baby was born, when there was some kerosene left. Now he only had one piece of newspaper, a handful of driftwood as kindling, and the logs which, until he bought his winter coal supply, were all that was available for the main blaze. It took nearly an hour to work up the full heat which he must have; and while he waited, he had plenty of time to wonder if this was the best way.

There could no longer be any question that it had to be done somehow.

He had often thought, before this evening, of just this problem; there was something about living alone on the river—itself a prime disposal area—and listening on the radio to almost daily accounts of holdup men bursting in, and hit-and-run motorists with a dead body on their hands, and quarreling couples who fought a little too hard, and drunken New Year's Eve parties ending with the skull fractured on the edge of the fireplace, and husbands returning too early, and wives too late, which always stimulated the imagination. It came down to a very precise question: What did you do if you had to get rid of a corpse?

For Carter, at this moment of near terror, the choice did not seem wide. There was burial in the garden, and the answer to that was no—there was always a passerby, a chance watcher to be feared, even at night. There was burial, or some other kind of hiding, inside the house; the answer could be yes, but it meant living with it, perhaps for the rest of your life; if you moved away, the new occupants started exploring, or they sold the house for demolition, or the big new road, with its deep foundations, was routed right through the cellar.

There was the river itself, but that was too chancy; it was a busy place, with boats (to the initiated) as recognizable as people, and it had a score of fisher-men dropping small anchors every day, hauling them in again when they wanted to move on, and perhaps coming up with the biggest catch of their lives.

There was plain butchery, the kind of thing which Jo-Anne Broom had loathsomely hinted at, with her talk of an electric carving knife. There were other solutions, which this same horrible girl had mentioned; the abandonment, the post-office trick, the carefree drive out into the country. . . . But they were all dangerous—and he had enough dangers crowding him already. He had not even begun to think of the worst threat of all—Joe Pepper the salesman, the sort of persistent, rubbery character who was bound to come back, who would keep on gossiping and perhaps fer-reting around, who might have to be outfaced with a plain lie (*there was no one here, I don't know what you're talking about*) which must somehow be made to stick.

But that was in the black future; this job was now. . . . Carter watched, sweating with more than the heat, as the fire in the furnace took hold, and built up a solid base of glowing ash. This really was the best way, for what had to be destroyed. It was only a baby, after all, a baby in a cardboard box labeled "Number One Son." It ought to be easy. It was so small.

It was small, but it wasn't easy. The fire kept fading

out, and before he could pile on more logs he had to find kindling to get them going. There was very little in the house; the real driftwood season, when he laid in stock for the winter, was still months ahead; this was not the time when innocent people started up their furnaces.

He found a wicker basket, which his wife had used for gardening, and the remains of an old deck chair, wrapped around with rotting canvas which made an acrid stench when he stuffed it into the fire. He chopped up a box which had once held soft drinks, and a broken picture frame, set aside for mending. But still the fire only just kept pace with what he wanted to do, what he must do.

The flames had licked away the "Number One Son" label, and the box itself had long ago burst open. The grisly object inside, now hidden by smoke, now partly exposed, was almost more than he could bear to see; and to pile fresh logs on it needed all his courage. Presently, when the fire seemed to be going better, he went upstairs, and then out into the front garden.

He sluiced his trembling hands at the river bank, and then, standing a few feet from the water's edge, sickened and afraid, he glanced back at the house.

Smoke was billowing from the chimney in a dark, slow-moving cloud which drifted gently downstream.

In mid-June, at the end of a hot day, it was the only smoke to be seen for miles around. It seemed to Carter, now under extreme tension, to be shouting his guilt out loud.

He turned back to the river, and immediately became aware that he was being watched, from a new angle altogether.

There was a boat at anchor, not more than thirty yards out; a small shabby outboard skiff with one man fishing from the stern. Carter knew the boat, and he recognized the man, in the same automatic way as could everyone else along the waterfront; the bright red T-shirt confirmed the green-topped, repainted Mercury outboard which always went with it. Together they belonged to an odd local character, not yet assimilated, known universally as Dr. Popski.

He was known as Popski because that was the nearest most people could come to his long Polish name, which certainly began with P and just as certainly ended in -ski. He was a middle-aged Polish immigrant who had lived and worked in the district for some two years. In the past, in the old country, he had been a doctor; now, lacking the right medical credentials, and being too old (he had once told Danny Frost) to pass any more examinations, he worked as a carpenter, and a good one.

When times were slack (and places like Stampville

were full of expert amateur carpenters who saw no need to pay another man $2.25 an hour to do something they would rather do themselves), Dr. Popski fished for his supper.

He was fishing now, but, Carter observed with quick misgiving, he was doing more than fishing. He was watching, in a curiously intent way, Carter and the house; now and then his head was cocked sideways, at a strange angle, as if—Carter could not decide what "as if" really involved. But Dr. Popski was certainly watching, with persistent, unobtrusive zeal; he kept glancing from Carter to the house behind him, and sometimes up to the chimney, and now and then at the smoke drifting low on the water; he was furtive and eager at the same time, as though he did not want to be noticed, yet could not afford to miss anything.

He looked like a man who knew something, and was going to stay and spy until he knew some more. . . . At that point, Carter pulled himself up sharply, realizing how wild and woolly his thoughts had become. This was his guilt thinking, not his brain; this was the morbid self-consciousness of a man with an unbearable secret.

Popski was not a spy, he was poor old Popski, trying to catch a few perch for supper, and in the meantime enjoying the view and the peaceful evening. . . . Carter threw off his fear with a real effort of will. If he was going to be scared by every shadow, every second glance, he would give himself away very quickly.

By and by he got down to work on some long-postponed chores, tidying up the dock, cleaning his boat out, brushing the spiders' webs from the eaves of the roof. Above his head, the smoke still billowed, steadily, lazily, drifting away down the river. He tried not to look at it, but he was glad at the thought of the furnace still burning, without interruption. Every minute it kept going was a minute nearer safety.

He stayed around the garden till after eight o'clock, when dusk came down and the dew began to fall. Popski, faithful fisherman, hungry man, also stayed where he was; if he were curious still, Carter did not want to know about it. When the shore lights began to come on, Popski laid aside his casting rod, and hauled in his anchor, and chugged slowly past the house on his way home. His head was still raised at the same inquisitive angle.

Carter waved to him, as most river folk waved to each other, and Popski waved back, though with a very small show of interest, as if, for some reason, he did not really want to make close contact with Carter. But that must be because he was a Pole, far from home, and shy, and poor, and not really part of the village. . . . His boat moved out of sight upstream, and the sound of its motor melted into the evening air.

Carter looked up at his roof. The smoke was dying away again, fading into a thin spiral. He must do a little more work on that. . . . He stacked the garden tools, and went quickly back into the house.

*

9

He was splitting fresh logs in the basement when he heard the short ring and then the loud double knock at the door. He paused, the ax raised for the next stroke, and listened; but the only sound was from the furnace, where the ash of the nearly dead blaze was dropping down through the fire-bars. He was not expecting anyone—he never expected anyone—and the harsh summons had not sounded like Danny Frost, nor anyone else he knew.

Carter could have ignored it, but already he was

terrified of doing anything out of the ordinary. People who did not answer the door always had something to hide. . . . The bell sounded again, a long determined ring which was not going to be denied, and he put down the ax, and went up the cellar steps, and opened the front door.

In the half light, he saw the uniform, and then he saw the man. It was one of Stampville's three policemen; Constable Tom Winnington. Behind him in the driveway was Stampville's only police car, with the red flashing light spilling over onto the front steps as it turned.

Carter's heart began to thud, while he strove his utmost to control himself and keep a normal expression. This might just be a social call, since he had talked to the other man often enough; Stampville's police force was housed in the town hall, and its members wandered in and out of the offices at will. But the timing was certainly brutal. . . . It was not made to seem less brutal when Tom Winnington said, with that mock-sternness which sometimes concealed a genuine readiness to push other people around:

"Hold it, Jack! Where's the fire?"

Carter looked at him for as long as he possibly could before answering; he was trying, at this appalling moment, to win back his self-control, and trying also, with desperate speed, to work out whether his caller was on duty, or off. Perhaps the law was never really off duty. . . . Tom Winnington was a tall man, like most policemen, and a little overweight from the beer and the snatched sandwiches which took the place of meals, and as cautious as any other man who had ten years' service behind him, and some promotion overdue, and another twenty years to go for his pension, whatever happened.

He had the reputation of being a good mixer, and honest, and not too smart or tough; just smart and tough enough for the job, the way country people liked their policemen to be. Carter had always thought of him as a friend, a casual friend. If he had suddenly become an enemy, how did one find out? How, without confessing, without showing a wound, without giving anything away, did a man with a half-burned corpse at his back discover whether Constable Tom Winnington was there by chance, or for a good official reason?

Whatever the reason, Carter could not delay the discovery any longer.

He must play it, he decided, as dumb as possible. If Tom Winnington could open with a stock police joke ("Where's the fire?" was what the speed-trap enforcers were always supposed to say), then he himself was free to spring an answer from the same silly book.

He said: "Sorry, officer. I was hurrying home before I had an accident."

Tom Winnington grinned, and it was a brief pleasure to see it. "Come on, Jack—you can do better than that. I mean, the real fire. We heard your chimney was making like the glue factory."

"Well, it's not." Suddenly, Carter felt a little braver; it was the only way to feel, under this kind of shock. "Is that on the level? Someone saw some smoke?"

"They sure did."

"Well, good for them. . . ." Carter leant sideways against the doorpost, trying with all his might for an easy attitude; the turning red light was strong enough to sound a continuous warning note, not strong enough to betray him. "I guess there was some smoke," he said reasonably. "I had the furnace going, earlier on."

"Why?" asked Tom Winnington, with a slightly rougher edge. He had been sniffing surreptitiously before; now he drew in a good hearty nose-full. "You got it going now?"

"Yes. Why not?"

"Well, it's June, isn't it? It's been hotter than hell, most of today. Who needs a furnace?"

"I was burning things," answered Carter.

"What things?" Now Tom Winnington was staring back at him; he was still the taller man, even though he was standing on a lower step; something about his air of alert authority told Carter that this was the key question. "What were you burning?"

"Gee, how should I know?" Carter tried to make a success of a slight touch of irritation. "Just kitchen trash. It was getting too much for the cook."

"What cook?"

"Me. The only cook there is. I missed the garbage man, last week."

"Wasn't he around, then?"

"Yes, he was around. I mean, I forgot to put some of the trash out. I forgot a whole pail-full." Too many details, an inner voice warned Carter; who really remembers garbage? But he had to complete what he had been aiming to say. "So I had a do-it-yourself garbage night. Coffee grounds, chicken bones, the lot."

"Oh. . . ." At the answer, Tom Winnington's face changed, as if he were beginning to see the light, and it was a light he much preferred to see. "You eating chicken these days?"

"That's against the law?"

"It's against the budget, as far as I'm concerned. Some people must be doing all right."

"Well, it was just once." Carter had a small stab of fear. He had not bought a chicken for months; it might be just the sort of thing they could check. "I picked up some of that barbecued stuff. . . . Hey, what *is* this?" he demanded suddenly. "Too much smoke, or something? Lots of people burn their trash. Better than throwing it in the river, messing it up, spoiling the fish."

"That's for sure. . . ." A good note had been struck, Carter knew; Tom Winnington was a keen fisherman himself. "Well, I was just checking," said the policeman. He was looking at Carter in a different sort of way; it was now a social look, not a disciplinary one. "Are you O.K. again?"

"Sure I'm O.K. Why not?"

"Mr. Blagdon was saying you had flu, or something."

"Oh, that. . . . I guess it was 'or something,' " Carter went on, man to man. "You know how it is. I just had to take Monday off."

Tom Winnington grinned, as Carter had intended him to. "Like that, was it? That's what Mr. Blagdon kind of hinted."

"I wouldn't doubt it."

"You must be living it up. Chicken *and* the hard stuff."

The interview had now changed a good deal of its character, but it was still going on, and that was the very last thing Carter wanted to happen. Tom Winnington still showed no signs of leaving; he was feeling in his breast pocket for a cigarette; the cluster of moths around the red flashing light had thickened till they were a solid whirling cloud, a permanent part of the scenery.

It was not possible to ask him to come in; it was not possible to send him away, even in the free-and-easy atmosphere of what the local radio station was fond of calling "Stampville and the river district—mainstream of Paradise." Even the mainstream of Paradise had laws, and policemen, and certain clear-cut local customs which dictated who was in charge and who was not.

Tom Winnington said: "You don't smoke, do you?" and lighted his own cigarette, completing the informal pattern. But he was still there, standing like a sentry on the steps, with the red light blinking and blinking to back him up. Carter had stopped feeling brave; some sort of reaction had set in, leaving him nervous and morbidly self-conscious. How did he look, how did the house look, was the smoke still rising, did it seem normal, did it smell right, was Tom Winnington satisfied or still suspicious?—the questions seemed to be setting up a flurry inside his head, like those damned insects whirling around the flashing light.

Within a few seconds, he knew at least some of the answers, and the flurry inside his head grew wilder, speeding up into something he could almost feel and hear. Tom Winnington, it was plain, was still there because he was still working. He hadn't finished his job, and, cigarette or no cigarette, he was staying on duty.

It started with an offhand question, one which plenty of other people put to him from time to time.

"Have you heard from your wife lately?" asked Tom Winnington.

"Oh, yes," answered Carter.

"Still away, eh?"

"Yes. She's staying with her sister, out in California somewhere."

"Somewhere?"

"They've got one of those big house trailers. They keep moving around."

"But you've heard from her?"

"Sure."

Tom Winnington said, much more bluntly: "They say there was a girl here."

Carter had to think very quickly. A brush-off for a little squirt like Joe Pepper was one thing; a straight lie to a policeman was something else again. He could not even guess how much Tom Winnington knew, but it could be very, very dangerous to say "No girl" if there were any evidence to the contrary. It could open up all sorts of things; it could end by bringing him down completely. . . . He had to show part of his hand, in order to save the rest.

To win himself a moment longer, he asked curtly: "Who says so?"

"These things get around," answered Tom Winnington, and gave him a straight stare. "True?"

"Yes," said Carter after a moment. "Yes, there was a girl here."

Tom Winnington sighed, as if he had not really wanted to hear this, as if he were disappointed, not pleased, with what he had extracted. "Well, well. . . . You really *are* living it up, aren't you?"

"I'm not living it up at all," answered Carter stoutly. "It wasn't that sort of thing."

"Who was the girl, then?"

"Someone I gave a lift to. On the road. She was hitchhiking."

"So?" The tone was decidedly bleak.

"She hadn't anywhere to go. So she stayed a couple of nights."

"A *couple* of nights?"

"Well, maybe more. . . . She was flat broke. . . . Look, Tom, I know it sounds funny, but that's absolutely all it was. She was broke, and I let her stay. . . . What was I to do?—just kick her out? You wouldn't do that to a dog. . . . In the end, I gave her some money, and she took off."

"How much money?"

"All I had in the house. Maybe five dollars."

"Pretty girl?"

"Not even that."

"M'm. . . ." Tom Winnington seemed inclined to believe him; Carter was, in fact, a very unlikely candidate for disbelief, in this area. But the subject was not closed. "Kind of a silly thing to do, wasn't it?"

"I don't see why."

Tom Winnington shrugged, rather irritably. "Well, your wife's away. Been away a long time. Suddenly there's a girl in the house. You know how people talk."

"I didn't think of that."

"You ought to have more sense." The other man now sounded definitely annoyed, as if there were enough stupid people in the world without Carter joining the gang. "Picking up a girl on the road. . . . You were taking a hell of a chance! Don't you know that?"

"I suppose so. I didn't think of it like that."

"Well, you'd better think of it. . . . You can get into all kinds of trouble. . . . Hell, don't you ever read the newspapers? There are stories every day."

"But you've got to help people."

"Not like that, you haven't. You pick up enough hitchhikers, you end up in the morgue. Some of these people are on the run. They're tough!"

"I suppose so," said Carter again.

Tom Winnington relaxed, and smiled briefly. "And if you pick up enough girls, you get yourself a reputation." But he was throwing away his cigarette; he seemed, at last, on the point of leaving. "O.K., Jack— I guess that's it. Just let the girls alone, heh?"

"I'll do that."

"And keep that smoke down."

"O.K."

This really was the end, and Tom's next remark clinched it. Turning away towards his car, he asked:

"When are we going to get you to come bowling?"

Carter smiled. "I wouldn't be any good. I hear the town hall team is hot."

"You heard wrong. . . . Honest, you ought to try it some time. It's a lot of fun."

"I wouldn't know the first thing about it."

"You don't know what you can do till you try."

Tom Winnington was opening his car door, and Carter felt so happy about his leaving, so confident, that he asked one extra question, one too many.

"How did this all start, anyway? About the smoke, I mean."

The motor sprang to life as Tom Winnington turned the switch. Above its beat, the answer was clear enough:

"Some nut called us up."

*

10

Some nut. . . . It had only taken these last two words to put Carter into a worse state of shock than he had known during the whole of the last ten days. They struck a violently false note, threatening to bring him face to face with extreme danger. When he went back into the sitting room, and sat down, he found that he was trembling beyond control.

Some nut. . . . Why had Tom Winnington used that particular phrase? You didn't have to be a nut to object to excessive smoke, or to report a chimney on fire; not unless the report had been, in some way, right out of line—unless there had been tacked onto it something so odd that it had aroused police curiosity. What had "some nut" said on the telephone? Why was he now classified as a nut? And why had he phoned the police, anyway, instead of the fire station? What had *really* brought Tom Winnington to Carter's front door?

He had said something about a glue factory. What had prompted that strange image? Then, at the end, he had dismissed the whole thing as the idea of "some nut." Once again, why? What sort of idea could it have been, to earn that label? It could only mean that some nut (Carter was sure that it was Dr. Popski, for no good reason except that he had been the last watcher near the house)—that some nut had phoned in a story so wild that it had brought the police running. What sort of story had it been? And what had killed it?

Carter sat back on the sofa, hopelessly out of his depth, without the strength to swim a stroke. He had no clues—or, if there were clues, he was not smart enough to see them. Wearily he closed his eyes. He was not smart enough for anything. He knew also, at that deadly moment, that he was not brave enough, either—not brave enough to go down to the cellar, and start up the furnace again.

It was too dangerous. It was too horrible. It would have to wait till tomorrow; very early tomorrow morning. . . . He *must* get some sleep. . . . If he didn't get some sleep, if he didn't somehow work himself free of all the things that were battering at him. . . .

In the end he fell asleep in his clothes, on the sofa, and dreamed frightful dreams, and woke at dawn with all the lights still on; woke sweating, tense, and afraid, to the day's disgusting task.

He came to life as slowly as he could; there would be nothing about this day which would make it less than dreadful; it was a day which he must somehow work through, and cover up, and push out of the way forever, in the hope of better ones to come. . . . He shuffled out to the kitchen, and made himself some coffee, and watched, as he drank it, the cold dawn light gaining strength, creeping towards him across the river, revealing him more and more.

The sunrise itself was clouded over, dull as routine, dull as pain; nothing sparkled, nothing drew new life from it, nor hope either. . . . Presently he dumped the coffee things into the sink and, bracing himself, went slowly down the steps into the cellar.

In the fearsome job of raking out the fire and preparing a new one, he found that there was still far more to do than he had hoped. He would have given anything to be able to leave it till evening, but he did not dare to. He had a picture of Tom Winnington coming back, with the house empty, and getting inside, and starting to poke around. . . . The police could always get into houses, and find excuses for it afterwards. . . . There was only one answer, and it must be faced; this thing had to be finished before he left for the town hall, in less than two hours' time.

He set to work, fighting back his nausea, trying to deaden his mind to everything except the crucial job of disposal. He was doing terrible things; but unless he did them, other people would do terrible things to him. . . . When all was ready, he set a match to what was now a solid bonfire, and watched the flames take hold, and then, sickened beyond endurance, he went upstairs again.

Standing at the front window, he looked riverwards. It was full daylight now, and the smoke which was beginning to drift across the water was billowing into a clear signal, a positive beacon. But at least it meant that the fire was going full blast. . . . Then he saw, with terrible alarm, that at one edge of the smoke there was a boat anchored, with a man fishing from it.

It was "some nut" again—Carter was now sure that this was he; Dr. Popski, with red T-shirt, green outboard motor, head alert, eyes watchful—exactly and fatally the same as on the previous evening. Even as he looked, Popski reeled in and laid aside his casting rod, and stood up in the boat, and began staring directly at Carter's roof, without disguise.

Carter felt panic begin to take hold, like a pair of wrenching hands at his throat. Nothing that he was doing was a secret anymore. . . . He watched, in fascination, while Dr. Popski continued his survey, his head turning this way and that, his face lifting, like a questing hound which had the scent and wanted the quarry. . . . Carter was not at all surprised, only terrorized afresh, when Popski sat down again, and quickly hauled in his anchor-line, hand over hand, and sped away upstream at the fastest clip his old outboard motor could make.

Carter almost ran from his observation post, and tore down to look at the furnace, frantically seeking some way to check it. But there was nothing to be done about the flame, nor the smoke either; the bonfire he had so carefully built could not be put out; it must be allowed to burn through to the end. When he had made up his mind to this, he went upstairs again, nearly crying under the grip of fear, and looked, from long-continued habit, at the clock.

It was past seven already. Whatever was going on, he *must* leave this, he *must* straighten up, and shave, and go to work, without any margin of delay.

He was barely ready to leave the house, and still panting and shivering from the effort to concentrate, instead of doing what he ached to do—lie down, and cover himself from the world, and sleep forever— when noises, and voices, and presently an echoing ring summoned him to the front door.

Carter had known, somewhere inside him, that it would be Tom Winnington again. But he could not have guessed that it would be Dr. Popski as well.

He had never met the other man, nor seen him closer than across the width of a street; and Popski face-to-face was a very different person from Popski at a distance, Popski waving casually from a boat. He was a small, slight man—so much, Carter had known already; but he had not known the sort of face and bearing he had—a face lined and seamed by the deep carving of care, a face full of suffering and compassion; the face of a man who had brought to his new country, for unguessable reasons, a great load of worry which must have lasted many years, and would last many more.

He was like a very strange painting, thought Carter in an instant of frightened recognition, or a very good photograph by a true artist of the camera: "Portrait of a Man Remembering"—something like that. He was standing on the lower step, beside Tom Winnington, completely dwarfed by the policeman, and yet dwarfed only in size; in quality, in the seasoning of life, he was no man's inferior.

Together, they were a most formidable couple; and they were made more formidable still by their bearing—the policeman as tough and confident as oak, the small immigrant wildly excited, bursting with something which must be information, knowledge, the inside story. . . . Carter had no time to sort out these astonishing, light-headed thoughts before Constable Tom Winnington spoke.

"Morning, Jack. I'm glad we caught you."

The innocent yet hateful word in that sentence hit Carter very hard. What could "caught" mean, except what it *really* meant? . . . But he had a few gasping efforts yet to make, and he did the best he could, summoning up all that was left of a shattered spirit.

"Hello, Tom. . . . You're up early. . . ." Then he looked at Dr. Popski, and nodded briefly, Stampville-fashion. "Hi, there. . . . What's the trouble?"

Tom Winnington said: "Jack. . . . What's all this smoke again?"

Carter reacted as firmly as he could. "It's smoke, that's all it is. I've got the furnace going, like I told you last night. Same thing. . . . There's no law against that, is there?"

"Take it easy," said Tom Winnington. But he did

not sound as if he cared whether Carter took it easy or not. "I'm just making inquiries, that's all."

Dr. Popski spoke suddenly. He had a small, rasping voice, and an accent which somehow went with his face; as if both accent and face had been fashioned inch by inch, with great labour and endurance. "You are burning something," he said. "You should tell us precisely what it is."

"What *is* this?" asked Carter loudly, making an enormous effort to sound surprised. "What the hell's going on? Why should I tell anyone about anything?"

"There's been another complaint about the smoke," said Tom Winnington.

"So what?" Carter countered savagely. "It's *my* house, and I'm burning *my* garbage in *my* furnace!" He jabbed his thumb towards Popski, with the kind of contempt which he knew was all wrong. "What's it got to do with him, anyway?"

"You do not answer the question precisely," said Popski, unmoved, as if what he knew was strong enough to withstand any insult, any counterattack. "This was my prophecy."

"What's that supposed to mean, for God's sake? I don't have to tell you a thing!"

"Sorry, Jack," said Tom Winnington—and he really was strong now, strong and determined, not to be put off by any brand of double-talk. "It's not as easy as that. . . . I want to take a look around. D'you mind?"

The whole thing was running out like bath water, and the whole world with it; but Carter still tried, perhaps for the last time, to reverse the flow.

"Of course I mind!" he said violently. "Why shouldn't I mind? Hell, I was just going to work! . . ." He looked from Tom Winnington to Dr. Popski, the shabby and absurd figure with the face of high quality and the cheap red T-shirt which completely belied it. "What I want to know is, I want to know—"

"Jack," said Tom Winnington, interrupting a sentence which Carter could never have finished properly, however hard he tried, "this isn't getting us anywhere, is it?" He mounted the top step; he really was coming in, and this was what he said next. "I'm coming in," he told Carter. "Whether you like it or not. . . . So just you stand aside."

"I warn you—" Carter began, though feebly.

"Don't warn me," said Tom Winnington, with sudden grimness. "Just make way. We're going to clear this up, right now."

*

11

Carter watched in miserable fear as the policeman went to work. First he took a pail of water, and dowsed the fire bit by bit; the cloud of filthy-smelling smoke which filled the cellar set them all coughing, but it did not stop Tom Winnington. He produced a small flashlight, and held it in his left hand while he took up a garden rake with the other; then he began, as the smoke cleared, to probe very gently and carefully through the ash and the half-burned wood.

Both Carter and Dr. Popski had to watch him as he worked; they could not have done anything else. Popski was peering over the policeman's shoulder into the furnace; his breathing was laboured, as if he had run a long way to meet this assignment, and in his face was the same kind of horrified excitement as one saw in the faces of people watching other people trapped in burning buildings, or boxers being murdered in the ring, or men drowning a few feet from the shore.

Carter did not want to watch; he wanted to die. But he was being forced, by some kind of hateful, self-mauling fascination, to stare into the furnace as Tom Winnington raked it out; even though he knew what must be discovered, even though he was watching his own doom. When the rake moved to and fro, it was moving across his own body, scraping his own raw flesh. But he had to watch it, and feel it also.

It was a link in the chain which he himself had forged, from that moment when he stopped his car and asked: "Want a lift?" It was part of the beginning of the end of the story. He had to watch it, just as he had to act it out to the very end.

The smoke thinned and cleared. Tom Winnington explored deeper and deeper, tipping aside half-charred logs, combing across the softer ash. Dr. Popski had a look on his face which might have been prayer, could have been appetite, while Carter was staring into the furnace as if his whole life hung on this act of witness.

Then there came a moment when the policeman suddenly stopped working, and simply gazed at what he had done. He drew in his breath with a sharp hissing sound, as if, at last, humanity had taken over from the machine. He was looking into the dead fire, as Carter looked, and Popski looked, in equal fear and astonishment.

In the heart of the grey-black, sodden ash, a small skull was now exposed; and then, as the flashlight trembled and moved, all the rest took shape, in tiny, pitiful detail.

Tom Winnington said: "Christ! It's a kid!" and Popski, pressing himself closer, exclaimed: "I knew it! I knew it! This was my prophecy! I told you. I had terrible dreams last night. But a child!" Then the policeman dropped the rake with a harsh clatter, and whipped around on Carter.

"What *is* this?" he demanded, in a loud, brutal voice. "What the hell's been going on?"

"What you see," answered Carter. He could only whisper; a sick terror had overtaken him, bringing him close to fainting. "I'm sorry, Tom."

"*Sorry!*" Tom Winnington's voice set up an iron echo in the close space of the cellar. "You must be—"

He broke the sentence off, as if there were not a word in the world to fit it. "Talk," he said grimly. "And talk sense, for God's sake! What's been happening here?"

"Can we go upstairs?" asked Carter. His head was spinning, and the tainted smoke was still thick and sour in his nostrils. "I don't feel well."

"O.K.," said Tom Winnington, after staring at him for a moment. "Get going." He gave Carter a light push towards the cellar steps. "And Jack—"

"What?"

"Don't fool around. I'm right behind you."

Upstairs, Carter sat down immediately, and dropped his head into shaking hands. But within a moment he had to look up again; this thing would not disappear, nor change into something else; it had all happened.

The policeman stood towering above him, in front of the fireplace; now that the first angry shock was over, he seemed different, perhaps more of a friend, more like Tom Winnington again. But he was still the police, armed and alert and possessed of all the hideous facts. . . . It was Dr. Popski who went through into the kitchen, and brought a glass of water, and said: "You should drink this," as he held the glass up to Carter's lips.

Carter drank, the glass rattling against his teeth. His head was clearing, in the cleaner air upstairs; he was not going to faint or die; now he was only trapped, only ruined. . . . He glanced up at the clock, close behind Tom Winnington's massive shoulder.

It was nearly eight already. He would be late for work. Blagdon would be on to him straightaway, he would—Carter had forgotten that people like Blagdon couldn't matter much any more. He sipped at the water again, and said "Thanks" as Dr. Popski took the glass away.

"O.K.," said Tom Winnington, who had not stopped staring down at him. "Now let's have it."

Carter found that he could begin immediately; he had only the truth to protect him, and the truth must pour out as swiftly as possible, and carry some of this terrible moment away with it. Otherwise he would indeed be damned. . . . He sat back on the sofa, and looked up at Tom Winnington, the enemy, and started the small beginnings of a fight for life.

"I told you about the girl," he said, "the one that stayed here. But I didn't tell you everything. She was having a baby. . . . She had it here, and it died. Then she just took off. . . . That's all there is."

"What d'you mean, that's all there is?" asked Tom Winnington harshly, after waiting a moment. "It's not even the beginning. It doesn't explain a thing."

"I mean, about the baby. It had nothing to do with me. That's what I meant."

"So?"

"So I didn't know what to do with it. . . . It was just *left* here. . . . So I—" he gestured "—you know. It was the only thing to do."

"It *wasn't* the only thing to do! Even if this is true, it was the *worst* thing to do! You must have been out of your mind!"

"I know," said Carter. "Maybe I was. I just couldn't think of anything else."

"So you put it in the furnace."

"Yes."

"But people don't *do* things like that!" Tom Winnington's voice had an odd, scandalized tone; obscurely, Carter felt a moment of pride that at last he had managed to surprise someone. And a policeman too. . . . "Why in hell didn't you report it, the same as anyone else would have done?"

"I was scared. I didn't think anyone would believe me. I was afraid there'd be a lot of talk."

"You think there isn't going to be a lot of talk now?"

"I know *now*," Carter agreed hopelessly. "But *then*, I thought it would work out."

"Well, it didn't work out," snapped Tom Winnington. "It didn't work out, one little bit. . . ." He was looking at Carter with exactly the kind of look which Carter had hoped to prevent, as if what he had heard just didn't add up; as if there had to be more to it than this, if only to justify the past hour of search and exposure. "You know," he said at last, "I don't think you're like that at all. . . . I don't think you're the sort of person—" He broke off, suddenly cautious, as though it were dead against the handbook to show his line of reasoning. He said only: "If you'd told the truth, people would have believed you. Right?"

"I don't know about that," said Carter, aware of a danger not yet clear.

"Well, I do," countered Winnington. "Hell, everyone knows you, you've got a reputation. . . . That's what doesn't make sense. . . . Hell!" he exclaimed again. "I'm a friend of yours! Why didn't you tell me about it? Did you think I wouldn't believe you?"

"I told you, I was scared," said Carter, as obstinately as he dared. "It's such a funny story."

"You're damned right it is."

"And I didn't want a lot of talk. I didn't want people hanging around here."

"Why would they hang around?"

"I mean," said Carter, confused, "I mean, it would never stop, would it?"

"What wouldn't stop?"

"People hanging about. People looking around. Tramping all over."

"Why would that matter?"

"I don't like it, that's all."

"Why not?"

"You know the way I live," said Carter, trying for a different note. "Quiet. It suits me. I don't want a lot of people—it would never stop."

"So you keep it all a secret, and try to burn a body. . . . Is *that* ever going to stop? What's worse than this?"

"I told you, I just didn't work it out."

"I believe him," said Popski's voice suddenly.

He had been silent for so long a time that they both swung around to look at him. He was sitting by the window, listening intently; the carved face, framed by the mass of gray hair, was a picture of careful, straining concentration. Carter had not been counting him in, even as a spectator; he had had a vague idea that the other man couldn't be following all this properly, that his English would not be good enough to cope with the to-and-fro of the argument with Tom Winnington.

But it seemed that Dr. Popski was much more at home here than he looked and sounded, that he might even prove to be a friend worth having. Carter was about to say something—a word of thanks, a word of appeal—when Tom Winnington broke in.

"How's that?" he asked curtly.

"I believe him," said Dr. Popski again. "There is a similar scene in the opera *Europa auf Brenner Sattel.*"

"For heaven's sake—" began Winnington.

"It is not well known," said Popski. "By Benedetto di Pozza, the last pupil of Verdi. But in German. There was here a young girl—"

"Look, doctor," said Tom Winnington, almost snarling. "Just shut up, will you?"

"I try only to help," said Popski.

"Don't. Leave the help to me." He turned back to Carter. He was looking tougher suddenly, as if the interruption had not been useful to Carter at all, as if Tom Winnington had seen in it some kind of smoke screen, contrived to make a fool of authority. . . . "Let's get a few things straight," said the policeman, much more roughly than before. "There's some things that don't fit. . . . Let's hear some more about the girl, for a start."

"I don't know anything about her."

"How long was she here, then?"

"Ten days."

"Then you know something about her. . . . *Ten* days? Didn't you tell me, two days?"

"I said, it could have been a bit longer. That was before all this came out, anyway."

Tom Winnington looked at him in sardonic disbelief. "Maybe it's just as well we're both keeping track. . . . Which is going to be the truth? Then or now?"

"Now."

"O.K. Let's stick to that. And let's start again. . . . So she was here for ten days. Somewhere in the middle of that, she had the baby. Right?"

"She was here for nine days," said Carter, with painstaking care. "Then she had the baby. Then she left, after two more days."

"That's eleven days. . . . Where did she go to?"

"I don't know."

The policeman sighed. "Let's start *again*. Where did she come from?"

"I don't know that, either."

"Then what *do* you know about her?"

"Honestly, nothing at all." Carter spread out his hands helplessly. "That's why it's all so stupid. First she was here, then she was gone." That echoed something which Jo-Anne Broom herself had said, and he hated to remember it. He hated to remember even her name. "I didn't even get her name," he said.

"She was here eleven days, and you didn't get her name?"

"No."

"What did you call her?"

"Nothing. We—we didn't talk much."

"You're not talking much now."

It was true about Tom Winnington's new tough-ness, thought Carter in sudden panic. But it couldn't really be new; people didn't change all that amount. It must mean that Tom wasn't what they all thought; he wasn't easygoing and simple, he wasn't country-style at all. He was quick-witted and determined. He was clever, and he wasn't going to give up on this. . . . Carter found himself beginning to hate the other man, whom he had thought of as a friend, a coffee break colleague, in and out of the town hall offices. That wasn't what Tom Winnington was like. . . . He was like what he was now; full of questions, full of quick answers, sure of his memory, disbelieving. It must be the police training—and that wasn't a comforting thought, either.

"I can't help not talking," said Carter after a long moment. "There's nothing to tell you."

"We'll find that out. . . . Let's see where we are now. . . ." Tom Winnington tapped his forefingers together as he made his separate points. "You picked the girl up on the road. You let her stay here. She was going to have a baby. She *had* a baby. She—no, let's talk about the baby. What happened there? Who was the doctor?"

"There wasn't a doctor," said Carter. "She wouldn't have one."

"*Exactly!*" said Dr. Popski, in a sudden explosion of agreement.

Tom Winnington rounded on him. "How's that?"

"I am so sorry," answered Popski, aware of disapproval. "But this is the classical dilemma. In this opera of which I have spoken—"

"Cut that out!" Tom Winnington snapped at him. Then he woke to the fact that he was speaking to a much older man who was not without his own distinction. He might be a Polish immigrant, but he was a bit more than that. . . . "Look, doctor," he said, halfway between apology and irritation, "just give it a rest, will you? I'm letting you stay on here because you're a witness. But that doesn't mean—"

"I understand," said Dr. Popski. He gave a formal, slightly absurd bow in the direction of the policeman. "I will no longer interrupt."

"O.K." Tom Winnington turned back to Carter. "Where were we?" he asked, with a false air of effort. But he knew exactly where they were; there was no doubt at all about that. "The doctor," he answered himself, after the smallest possible pause. "Why didn't you get a doctor? Every girl having a baby needs a doctor."

"She wouldn't have one."

"You mean, you did it all?"

"Yes." Carter could hardly believe it now. "That was what she wanted."

It seemed that Tom Winnington could hardly believe it, either. "Well, well," he said, in a very unpleasant way. "You do a bit of everything, don't you? . . . What do you know about delivering babies?"

"Nothing."

"Is that why it died?"

"No, no! It was perfectly all right, to start with. Then it seemed to—it just began to fade out."

"Why didn't you get a doctor *then?*"

"Because she wanted to keep it a secret."

"A *baby* a secret? Why? Wasn't she married?"

"She said not," answered Carter. Then he passed his hand wearily across his eyes. The pressure was beginning to take effect; some of these blows were striking home; within a little while, he would be losing this game. "I mean, she said she was. But the baby wasn't her husband's." He tried to meet the policeman's eyes boldly, and failed. "She told a lot of different stories," he mumbled.

"Is that so?" said Tom Winnington sarcastically. "I hope it isn't catching. . . . Was it your idea, not to have a doctor?"

"No. I wanted to. But she wouldn't listen to me."

"You could have called one anyway. If you'd *really* wanted to."

"It wasn't like that. This was something she'd made up her mind to."

"How old was she?"

"Seventeen."

Even the policeman was surprised. "Hell's bells!" he said. "How old are you?"

"Forty. Well, forty-one."

"And you were letting a kid of seventeen call the shots? Not getting a doctor when she was having a baby? . . . Are you sure you didn't know her before? Like, about nine months ago?"

"No."

"But you won't give me her name?"

"I don't know it."

"Or where she came from?"

"I don't know."

"Or where she went?"

"I don't know."

Tom Winnington asked suddenly: "Is she still here?"

"No!" Carter shouted, goaded beyond all available endurance. "I tell you, she went away!" He looked at the policeman with hatred. "Why did you say that?"

"Well, the baby's still here, isn't it?"

A complete, startled silence fell between them all

as Tom Winnington's last sentence, with its terrible implication, was brought out into the open. Yet the impact on Carter was not to make him afraid, but to make him more angry. He could not see what Tom Winnington was trying to get at, except in terms of insult and provocation. The policeman already had his case; Carter had told him everything. Why was he keeping up the intolerable pressure?

What was the reason for this deeper probe, this continual hinting that the full story was far worse than it had seemed so far? Carter did not know the answer; but he did know one thing—that enough was enough, that he had told all he had to tell, that just because a man was a policeman—

He spoke the first thing that came into his mind, and he spoke it violently:

"The baby's still here because it's dead. You know that!"

"I know *that*," answered Tom Winnington, not at all affected by rebellion. "I know it for a damned good reason. Because I found it out. I found *it*. Now we've got a girl missing. Any ideas on that?"

"I don't know what you mean. Leave me alone!"

"I'll leave you alone when I've finished with you. . . . You know just what I mean. You told me there wasn't a baby here. But there is. You told me the girl went away. Well, *did* she go?—and if she did, why, and where to? And if not—" he glared suddenly at Carter, pressing it all home "—let's hear what really happened to her."

"Nothing happened to her!" said Carter, in furious agitation. "She just went away."

"All right. Let's move on to that bit. What was she wearing when she left?"

Desperately Carter tried to remember his first image of Jo-Anne Broom. "A dress. Sort of gray. And a loose coat. Like a rain coat."

"Then you saw her go?"

"No. I told you, she left in the middle of the night."

"You didn't tell me that. But it doesn't help you much, does it? If it was the middle of the night, how do you know what she was wearing?"

"I meant, those were the clothes she had on when she arrived." Memory jogged him sharply and painfully; there were some clothes of his wife's missing. Jo-Anne could have been wearing those. She could be wearing them still. Or she could have sold them somewhere, leaving all sorts of clues.

They might help to trace her, which could take care of some of his problems; but she might also claim—which was half true—that the clothes had been given her; and the police would ask why. He could hear them doing it, in Tom Winnington's voice: *"Why did you give your wife's clothes away to a girl you picked up on the road?*" The questions, like *these* questions, would never stop. Better leave the clothes out altogether. . . . "I took it for granted—" he started again.

"Let's not take anything for granted," said Tom Winnington. "We might get all tied up again, mightn't we? . . . A gray dress, and a rain coat. Any luggage?"

"Yes. She had a suitcase."

"How do you know *that?*"

Carter's head was beginning to spin again. "I mean, there was a suitcase missing after she left."

"Anything else missing?"

"No."

"You mean she took an empty suitcase?"

This was the matter of the clothes again; it was something Carter dared not open up. His brain wasn't working any too well, but he had to think of something very quickly. "She took some food."

"Like what?"

"How do you mean?"

"Food," said Tom Winnington, with heavy-weight sarcasm. "The word you used. F-O-O-D. . . ." He was right on top of this now; it seemed that he was strong enough to pull out of Carter's head anything that might be hiding inside. "What food did she take? Bread? Cheese? Meat? Half a chicken? Something in the fish line? Spaghetti and meat balls? A jar of pickles? You said she took a suitcase full of food. What food did she—"

"She took everything there was!" shouted Carter. He felt he would go insane if he could not put a stop to the rush of questions.

"O.K. What's everything?"

"Everything in the icebox."

"What's everything in the icebox?"

"Oh God!" said Carter, nearly screaming under the raw coercion. "How do I know? How can I remember? She's been gone for over a year!"

"That's what *you* say," said Tom Winnington easily.

Oh God, said Carter, this time to himself. *Let him miss it.* . . . He felt himself grow ashen pale, and start to sweat, as the awful self-betrayal hit him. It had been his runaway tongue speaking of its own accord, lured onto the wrong track by the thoughts of the stolen clothes. It was one of those fatal mistakes you were supposed to make when you were guilty, the kind of slip that told the truth, the kind you could only cover up if you—

"She took a lot of stuff for sandwiches," he burst out, at a furious gabble. "And a bit of corned beef, and hard-boiled eggs, and some—"

But the policeman had headed him, after all. "Hold on!" he commanded, in the sharpest voice he had yet used. His eyes now bore down upon Carter without mercy, in the very coldest inspection. "She's been gone for *how long?*"

All he could do was try to run over it. "Two days," said Carter.

"But you said, over a year."

"I meant, two days."

"Then why did you say, over a year?" The policeman's glance was almost impossible to endure. "Who's been gone over a year?" They both knew the answer; it was only Carter who could not bear to give it. "It's your wife!" said Tom Winnington, after an astonished pause. "Who said anything about your wife?"

"No one," answered Carter. He had to lick his lips; he could not have formed any words otherwise. "I wasn't thinking. It was just a mistake."

"But why make it? . . . We were talking about the girl, not your wife. . . . Don't tell me. . . . How long did you say she's been gone?"

"Two days."

"Which one is this?"

"Jo-Anne. I mean, the girl."

On Tom Winnington's face there was something between a grin and a snarl. "You know, you're not doing so well. . . . So now it's Jo-Anne. . . . What's the rest of her name?"

"Jo-Anne Broom. I just remembered. She did tell me."

"It's not so hard to remember," said the policeman, "once you get into the habit. . . . Jo-Anne Broom. . . . Let's see, she's the one that's been gone two days. . . . And your wife—how long did you say?"

"A year," said Carter. "You remember that."

"I remember *now*," said Tom Winnington. "You kind of reminded me. . . . You must be separated, then?"

"Sort of."

"Sort of. . . . Where did you say she was living?"

"Out in California. With her sister."

"What's the address?"

"I don't know."

"But you said she wrote to you."

"They keep moving about. In a trailer. I told you."

"What's her sister's name?"

"Carter," said Carter.

"Now how can *that* be?"

"Sorry. I mean, Mansfield."

"Like the actress."

"What actress?" asked Carter in desperation.

"Jayne Mansfield. It's a name you think of. . . . I'd like to see one of your wife's letters."

"I don't keep them," Carter mumbled.

"What's that?"

"*I don't keep them!*"

"Why not?"

"Because we're separated. We had a quarrel. Lots of quarrels." He swallowed, trying to ease the grip on his constricted throat. "You might as well know. She's left me. She's not coming back."

"Why does she write, then?"

"She doesn't write very often," said Carter, after a long ticking pause.

"That I can believe. . . . You know," said the policeman, suddenly slapping his hands together, "I think you're in a mess. One mess we know about. The one downstairs. The other—well, we'll just have to find out, won't we? I thought it was the girl, but I could be wrong. Maybe it's the girl *as well*. . . . I think," he went on, almost genial, "we'll take a big, big look around this house. And the garden. Is that O.K. with you?"

"I suppose so," said Carter. He had been so hammered and flattened during the last few minutes that he scarcely cared. He tried to summon the strength to resist, but it came out as feeble surrender. "Do what you want," he said at last, in a hoarse, exhausted whisper. "You won't find anything. . . . This is all crazy, anyway."

*

12

"Sure it's crazy," said Tom Winnington into the hand microphone. *"But it's true. Every word of it."*

Carter sat on the sofa in the middle of the room, dejected, on the verge of collapse, the very picture of defeat. The front door was open, and through it could be seen the police car standing in the sunlight, and inside the car, busy at the radio set which linked him to headquarters, the solid bulk of Constable Tom Winnington.

The policeman's voice could only be heard in snatches, and the answers to what he said came out as a series of muffled squawks, which Carter could not understand at all. But one side of the conversation was more than enough. . . . Though Tom Winnington was concentrating, and frowning, his sharp eyes were always fixed on the open front door. He was watching all the time; indeed, he never took his eyes off Carter for a second.

"You'll need the wagon anyway," said Tom Winnington.

Dr. Popski crossed the room, walking very softly, and laid a gentle hand on Carter's shoulder. Carter, who had not been expecting it—who had forgotten the other man altogether—jumped uncontrollably; but after a moment he managed to look up, and smile faintly in answer. At least he had one friend in the world, even though it was the friend who had first betrayed him. . . . He said, hopelessly:

"This isn't too good, is it?"

"Do not give way to despair," said Dr. Popski— and Carter wondered where Popski could possibly have heard, or read, or been taught that odd-sounding sentence. "They will believe you. I am sure of it."

"They won't," said Carter in a flat voice. He nodded

his head towards Tom Winnington, whose eyes still maintained their unblinking watch. "*He* doesn't believe me. It's going to be like that forever."

"Not so," answered Popski. He gave Carter's shoulder another touch of comforting pressure, and then sat down on the arm of the sofa. "But I would wish to say how much I regret making the start of this."

"That's O.K.," said Carter forlornly. "Maybe it would have happened anyway."

"At the same time," said Popski, "I make my apologies."

His voice was very gentle, very concerned; and his face, when Carter looked up at it, was full of such pity and kindness that it made Carter want to cry. If the world were all like this man, then it would be a better world. If *women* were all like this man—

"It's not your fault," said Carter. "Believe me, nothing's your fault."

"You are very good," said Popski.

"*I don't know who we're looking for,*" said *Tom Winnington, "but I'll bet it's someone.*"

The last words from the police car, from that sun-lit life outside which was proving so tough and treacherous, had been especially clear, and Carter could not shut them out, nor pretend that they had never been said. They were his death-knell, and he knew it. . . . Carter looked up at Popski, the grave and tender stranger who now seemed the only man of pity in the world. He thought that if he could only maintain this bridge, he might still have a chance. Or if not a chance, then an easier end to the awful day.

Suddenly he wanted to confess, to tell everything. But he did not want to confess to Tom Winnington —or rather, not *first* to Tom Winnington, his other friend who had turned into a bully, and was loving the change. He would rather tell it to this gentle man, the stranger-brother in the frayed red T-shirt who even now was saying:

"Do not fear. They will believe you."

"He better come out and take a look at the furnace, before anything's touched," said Tom Winnington.

"They will believe you," Popski repeated, with a certain passion of feeling. "There must be many such happenings every day! It is the wheel of fortune." Once again, in the midst of his intolerable fear and pain, Carter found himself wondering where such phrases came from. "Wheel of Fortune" was one of those damned tunes on the radio; he remembered Jo-Anne Broom saying disdainfully: "That's one wheel that really is fixed. . . ." "Tell the truth, and they will believe it," Popski went on. "The child died, the girl went away, and you were left with the problem. Tell them how it happened. There was no bad feeling. In the end, they will see that."

"You don't understand," answered Carter. The time had come when, at last, he was ready to share his terrible, year-long load of guilt and fear with someone else; and it need not be the tough, staring uniformed man whose mouth was talking into a microphone, but whose eyes were fixed unchangeably on himself. It could be this other man, whose face was the divine face of charity. "You don't understand."

"Tell me," said Popski.

"It's not the baby," said Carter, as manfully as he could. "It's not the girl, either—she did go away. It's —it's my wife."

"So," said Popski.

"She is here."

"So," said Popski, who seemed to have no use for the language of surprise, nor any taste for it. "How precisely is she here?"

Carter nodded his head towards the wide window looking onto the river. "Down by the dock."

"You mean, she is dead?"

"Yes."

"How long since?"

"A year," answered Carter. "The June before this."

Recalling the terrors of that summer night, which he had carried with him for so long, he shook his head in hopeless confusion. "Oh God!" he said, with all the anguish of man trapped by fate. "Why did this have to happen?"

"We'll need a work-gang," said Tom Winnington. "Spades, crowbars, the lot."

"We used to quarrel all the time," said Carter. "Not just quarrels—I mean, real fighting. At the end, she would always start to hit me. . . . I didn't make enough money, I wasn't any good, why weren't there any children, all that sort of thing. . . . I don't think it was my fault," he said seriously. "Even when she went off with someone, and he was such a big lover, there weren't any children either. . . . Then one night she came back from one of those trips, and we had the usual row, even though I hadn't complained about anything. I'd cooked my supper and done the dishes. . . . In the end she picked up an empty bottle, and hit me."

"So," said Popski again. His face, grave and lined and compassionate, was all that Carter could now see. It was like the face of a confessor, perhaps like the face of God. "This is a whole world of tragedy."

"She hit me just as hard as she could," said Carter. "I wasn't even standing up. . . . The bottle broke, and some of the pieces fell on the floor, in front of the fireplace." He was staring at the exact spot now, but it did not seem worth mentioning. "I lost my temper, and I hit her back, for the first time, *the very first time!* . . . It's the only time I'd been angry enough to do it. . . . She fell down, fell into all the broken glass, the big jagged bits."

He was still staring at the place of execution, remembering the thudding fall, and the terrible spreading stains which came after. "I was still so angry," he said, "I didn't even help her up. I just walked out. . . . I went out on the river in the boat, I cruised up and down for miles, thinking and wondering what to do. I just kept thinking this couldn't be all I was going to have, for the rest of my life. . . . When I came back, she was still lying there, but she was dead. . . . There was this big piece of glass, the bottom of the bottle, and it was stuck in her neck."

"O.K.," said Tom Winnington, "I'm bringing him in now."

"I'd been building a new dock, all that summer," said Carter. "I had to have something to do, to get out of the house. . . . There was a big trench this end of it, to pour the concrete for the steps—you know, to anchor the whole thing. So. . . . It was the only thing to do," he said. "It was the middle of the night.

Someone nearly saw me once, but I don't think they did. . . . I was scared to death all the time, but I had to go through with it." He looked up at Popski, perhaps for the last time, because the policeman was now climbing out of his car. "I know it sounds terrible, and I should have done it all different, I should have told them what happened. But *then*, it was the only thing to do."

"Like the child," said Popski.

"Just like the child." This man was turning out to be a very great comfort. It was unfair that he had arrived too late, that he was not going to have any say in all the things which were going to happen next. "That's something else which should have gone right, but it didn't. It just worked out wrong."

"I blame myself now," said Popski. "One should let such things sleep."

"How did you find out?" asked Carter. The colossal form of Tom Winnington was already looming through the doorway, preparing to take charge, preparing to put an end to all such secrets, all such innocent hopes. But Carter was beginning not to be afraid, or—what was perhaps the same thing, up and down the scale of life—not caring much about anything anymore. From now on, he need not even swim with this river; it would carry him on to the end, wherever that was, whatever he did. "I mean, it was you that got the whole thing going. Why was that?"

"I am so sorry," said Dr. Popski.

"But why?"

"The smoke," said Dr. Popski. There was a very curious look on his face, as if, after a long time of doubt, he still did not know whether to be proud or ashamed. "I smelled the smoke."

"I still don't get it," said Carter.

"I must therefore explain." The look on Popski's face was now changing subtly; neither pride nor shame seemed to be winning, but a kind of acceptance. Though it could not be of any help to Carter, he realized, with Popski's next words, that some enormity in the past was now relenting, or had begun, at last, to make sense. "It was for me a special smoke," said Dr. Popski. "You should understand, I was formerly with my family in Auschwitz."

DATE DUE